Lancaster Gate

Lancaster Gate

William Lyster

iUniverse, Inc.
New York   Bloomington

Lancaster Gate

iUniverse books may be ordered through booksellers or by contacting:

iUniverse
1663 Liberty Drive
Bloomington, IN 47403
www.iuniverse.com
1-800-Authors (1-800-288-4677)

ISBN: 978-1-4401-8942-5 (pbk)

ISBN: 978-1-4401-8943-2 (ebk)

ISBN: 978-1-4401-8944-9 (hc)

Printed in the United States of America

iUniverse rev. date: 11/25/09

Prologue

Tsuyoshi Akiba walked slowly past Tokyo's Imperial Palace Plaza and down the stairs to the Hibiya underground station. He dropped a token in the turnstile, passed through, walked a few yards along the tracks, and stood back along the wall to wait for the train.

He pulled a map and a piece of paper from an inside pocket, moved a few steps closer to the nearest light, and hurriedly read through the handwritten note as the train entered the station with a rush and rolled to a stop. There were no seats, as usual, but he didn't mind; it would be a short ride.

He got off at the second stop, walked through the Higashi-Ginza station and up the stairs. He barely glanced at the Kabukiza Theater as he walked back along Harumi Dori Avenue and stopped to look into the McDonald's window. It was crowded at this time of the morning, but a poster in a corner of the window reflected his image back to him: an ordinary face, a shaggy mass of black hair, a gray topcoat with both hands stuffed into the pockets.

He turned, continued on to the corner, turned right onto Chuo Dori Avenue, walked past Mitsukoshi department store, glanced at the entrance to the Ginza underground station, and paused at the next corner. He turned right and walked the short distance to the next corner, stopping before a very large store, Star Bright Cosmetics. Peering intensely through the window areas, which were extensively decorated with designer-label perfumes, makeup products, advertising posters, and skin-care products, he watched as three beauty consultants talked to customers on the right side of the store.

Cupping his hands on the glass and peering in, he was able to see counters along the left side of the store and what looked to be a curtain hanging in a doorway in the back wall, leading to what appeared to be an office or a storeroom. He entered the store and walked slowly toward the man who was standing near the curtain in the event that a customer was interested in products in the counters along the back wall.

Smiling broadly, he walked up to the man and asked, "Mr. Hirata?" After receiving a nod in reply, he said "I have a message from Marallon," and motioned toward the curtain.

Mr. Hirata turned, pushed the curtain aside, and stepped into the room. Akiba followed him, and as the heavy curtain fell back into place, he reached around Hirata, covering his mouth with his left hand. He pulled a gloved hand out of his right coat pocket and clicked the knife button. As the switchblade flashed out, he stabbed hard below the man's right ribs and then yanked out the blade. He reached around again, stabbing Hirata four times in the chest. As his muffled groan sounded, the man slumped forward.

The assassin pulled the knife out for the last time and eased the proprietor's badly bleeding body to the floor. He quickly wiped the bloody blade on the dying man's shirt, snapped it shut, turned, and pushed the curtain aside a few inches. He saw that the customers were still talking undisturbed and then pushed the curtain all the way open and walked leisurely through the store and out the front door. Walking briskly, he reached the corner, turned, and disappeared down the steps to the Ginza station.

Chapter 1

i

Kinya Arakawa, managing director of Marallon Japan, glanced down at the notes on his desk, took off his reading glasses, and looked around at his executive staff, seated in chairs in front of him.

Speaking quietly, he said, "The Mainichi police have finished their investigation of the murder of the Star Bright Cosmetics store owner. The report will be released to the press tomorrow, but since Star Bright was a major distributor of Marallon cosmetics, Inspector Matsumoto released an early copy to me today. It's taken quite a while, and they've done a very thorough job. But again—as in the previous two murders of cosmetic store owners—they have found no clues to the murder of Mr. Hirata at the Star Bright. The case is considered to be closed."

He hesitated, looked over at his secretary, who was taking notes of the meeting, and then continued. "The case will be carried as an open, unsolved murder, of course. The police investigated the family situation and found no reason to suspect anyone. Competitive retail stores are not of a size for the owners to have had any reason to want Mr. Hirata murdered. Robbery was not a factor. This crime was committed by stabbing, not strangulation with a Marallon scarf as were the prior two killings, as you recall."

He glanced around the group and said to the Tokyo sales manager, "Fukamiya-san, you'll be glad to hear that the police confirm your assessment that our salesman calling on the account was not in the vicinity of the store at the time of the murder and had absolutely nothing more than a casual business relationship with the owner of the Star Bright shop."

Turning to the marketing director, he noted, "Manufacturers of other cosmetics products sold in the Star Bright store cooperated fully with the investigation, and no reason to suspect implication of any of them was found."

Pausing, he sat back in his chair and then said, "This is the third time we've dealt with the murder of a major Marallon retail store owner in the past two years."

Glancing toward the personnel manager, he said, "None of our personnel files have revealed even a hint that anyone in our employ could be associated with these or any other crimes, but it seems to me that it's too much of a coincidence."

Standing up, he paced a few steps back and forth beside the desk. Running his fingers through his gray hair, he said, "From the facts as we've found them to date, it may be true that no one in our organization is implicated in any way, but I'm not convinced. Marallon has not had a situation like this anywhere else in the world. We conducted our own in-house reviews after each of the first two murders, with London's management assistance, and we've completed our own recent review since the third murder."

He paused, and his eyes swept across the faces of his staff. He continued, "But I'm still not satisfied. I've decided to ask Marallon U.S. to work out an arrangement for the London office to send an independent consultant to study our methods of operation. Perhaps an unbiased overview of the way that we do business, our everyday procedures, may reveal something that we've overlooked."

Sitting down in his chair again, he said, "I'll recommend that the consultant be given a thorough training course in UK operations and then come here to study us, to make sure that our methods are consistent with those of our London parent company, and to assure that we get an unbiased opinion."

Summing up, he continued, "The goal is not to find the murderer. The police have tried that three times and failed. The goal is to have an independent examination of our operations to see if there's anything that we're doing that contributed to the deaths of our three retailers and, if possible, to make sure there will be no way for any one of our people to become involved in such a tragedy in the future."

Looking at each individual in turn, he said, "That's all I have at the moment. If anyone has any questions, please wait. I'll try to answer them."

ii

On a train from Ramsgate, in the corner of a first-class smoking carriage, John McKay, a British consultant working for the London office of Worldwide Consultants, took a puff from his cigarette and ran an interested eye over the business news in the *Financial Times*. He laid the paper aside and glanced out of the window. His eye caught his reflection in the glass: the lightly tanned, well-shaved face of a thirty-year-old Englishman with light hair and somewhat shaggy eyebrows. They were slowing down for the stop at Canterbury. He looked at his watch—another two hours to go.

He thought again about what he'd been told had happened in the chairman's office at Worldwide Consultants headquarters one rainy May morning in Chicago. A vice president from the New York office of Marallon Cosmetics, having responsibility for the Japanese subsidiary, had discussed the murders of the retail store owners in Tokyo.

There was no direct relationship between the victims and the Marallon Company. Internal audits had found no connection with the murders, but the managing director was not satisfied.

Worldwide's chairman, Archie McClanahan's recommendation to detail a consultant from one of Worldwide's offices in Britain for an intensive course in Marallon UK operations, as a first step in reaching a satisfactory answer, was accepted by the U.S. company.

The first phase of the job had gone well. John had reported to Marallon's Ramsgate office, settled in at a temporary desk, and during the week met with headquarters' marketing and financial groups.

After information-packed working days, evening walks getting acquainted with the seafront toward Margate and then turning south toward Deal and the White Cliffs had been pleasant. Temporary lodging in the company flat at Broadstairs had been convenient, and the beach environment had been ideal for the hardworking bachelor, who had been detailed from Birmingham and was more than willing to brave the chilly breezes barreling in from the Channel.

It was stuffy in the smoking carriage. He unbuttoned his vest, ran a hand through his blond, wavy hair, and pulled down the knot of his tie, wishing he hadn't worn it since he was only on his way to a hotel.

From his jacket pocket, John took out a letter. The directions were clear.

Marallon House

New Bond St.

London, UK

Mr. McKay:

During your stay in London, you are to reside at a residential hotel near the company's Bond Street office. A reservation has been made for you at Beauregard House, on Gloucester Terrace, at Lancaster Gate. You are to report to Mr. Tim Campbell, our marketing director, at Marallon House at the top of New Bond Street on Monday, 17 June 2002, at 0900 hours.

Sincerely,

Philip Allbright

V.P. Administration

Marallon UK

John McKay looked up from the letter and tried to remember when exactly he had been to the West End. It must have been seven—no, eight years ago. He had visited London during his last year at graduate school in Birmingham and vaguely remembered Marble Arch, Speakers Corner, and Hyde Park with the lake in the center—was it the Serpentine?

It was Friday afternoon. He had the weekend to renew his acquaintance with that part of London. Refolding the letter, nodding his head in gentle approval of his recollection, John McKay allowed his eyes to close. He dozed.

iii

Madeline Claiborne, on a train from Brighton in a third-class carriage with three other travelers in it, leaned her head back and shut her eyes. She thought, *How pleasant it is traveling by train today! It'll be nice to get to London. Really a great piece of luck getting this job.*

When you wanted a photo modeling assignment it nearly always meant beach scenes at Brighton in a bikini, or posing with a new automobile or vacuum cleaner. For the professional model, cosmetics photo assignments were difficult to get, and landing one that involved a stay in London for an extended period of time seemed almost impossible. Even the agency hadn't held out much hope.

And then the letter had arrived.

Marallon House

New Bond St.

London, UK

Miss Claiborne:

As discussed during your interview, we have received your photo portfolio from the International Beauty Institute, which included the samples of your work with competitive beauty products. It is understood that you are available to stay in London for approximately one month while we complete photo sessions for a new product line introduction and a series of personal appearances in cosmetics sections at Harrods, Selfridges, and similar locations. Please report to Mr. Tim Campbell, marketing director, at Marallon House on Friday, 14 June 2002 at 0900 hours.

As agreed, reservations have been made for you at Beauregard House on Gloucester Terrace, at Lancaster Gate. Please take Thursday's 1240 train from Oakbridge station. You will be met at Paddington.

Sincerely,

Nancy Merlin

Assistant to Mr. Campbell

Suddenly, in spite of the pleasant temperature in the carriage, a warm flush crossed her face, and she wished she wasn't going on a close-up photo assignment. A picture rose clearly in her mind. Aaron, lying where he had fallen when the ladder tipped over, his arm and his smashed camera engulfed in flames beside the overturned oil lamps, and Madeline struggling to pull him back out of the flames but knowing, only too surely, that she wouldn't be able to save him.

She shuddered, put both hands to her forehead, covering her eyes, and took a deep breath. She dropped her hands back into her lap. She turned her head, opened her eyes, and frowned at the man sitting opposite her. He was an older man with a pale face, gray hair, and dark eyes fixed on her. Visibly concerned and with his mouth breaking into a slow smile as he looked into her eyes, he asked, "Are you alright, miss?"

Smiling, she said, "Yes, I'm fine. Thank you."

Recovering quickly and turning to look out of the window, she thought to herself, *He looks French. Probably just came in on the ferry from Dieppe.*

iv

Pierre Duval, sitting across from the woman he had just spoken to, thought to himself, *Quite attractive. Reminds me of Nicole just about the time we married, just after receiving my PhD from MIT.*

He frowned. His mind drifted back to his research project. He wished in a way that he hadn't agreed to do it now that he'd retired, but his work on nuclear instrumentation and radiation effects had established him as an authority, and he felt obligated to some of those who had known him at the Department of Energy.

Looking out the window at the English countryside, he thought that, as usual, it had been pleasant during the two weeks visiting his brother, who still lived in Dieppe, remembering his early teen years running messages for the underground and old times with other members of the Resistance right at the end of the war. He liked going back for the reunions every three years, and it was far easier making the trip since he'd become an American citizen, but the remaining members were getting fewer every time they met.

He didn't like being away from Nicole for two weeks, and the Channel crossing had not been smooth. Now the train was slowing for his stop at Haywards Heath. He had just two more days with Nicole at her sister's home not far from the station, and then they'd get back to Beauregard House at Lancaster Gate.

He'd be glad when he could sit down and move ahead with some new ideas. It was certainly fortunate that the terrorist attack on the Pentagon had not caused more damage.

He stood up, reached up to the overhead rack, put on his hat, and took hold of his briefcase and suitcase as the train rolled to a stop.

V

At Beauregard House, Susanna Brice, the hotel manager, stood casually at the reception desk and smiled to herself as Mrs. Brent moved slowly through the revolving door into the lobby.

"Did you find what you were looking for?" she asked the guest.

"Yes, I did find some brown shoes at Selfridges, but the prices are frightfully high," she replied as Susanna nodded.

It had been only a few days since Mrs. Brent had arrived from America with those four suitcases and her stated intention to stay indefinitely until she could decide where to retire. Actually, she was much too young to really retire. Her inheritance from Frank's estate had left her enough investments that she could stop working anytime; she really wasn't dependent on her salary. She had continued to work after Frank's death, primarily because she liked the work but also to keep her mind occupied and to close out the idea of a future without him.

She had been delighted when Susanna had thrown open a door at the end of a passage and led her into a pleasant bedroom with a big window that opened wide onto the rooftops of

William Lyster

Bayswater, reminding her of the rooftops of Paris. She had known many Brits during her years in Morocco with the American Peace Corps and had decided that London's climate would be more tolerable than those years of unbearable summer heat in Rabat. And she hoped residing in the UK would be more secure than living in a Muslim country

As Susanna turned to go, Mrs. Brent said, "I've been meaning to ask why you have so many small tables in the dining room."

Turning back, Susanna replied, "We try to assure our guests of personal privacy. You've probably noticed each of our single guests has a tendency to sit at the same individual table at every meal. It seems to help residents feel they're enjoying the privacy of their own homes but are free to engage the other guests in conversation, should they so choose."

With a smile and a nod, Mrs. Brent started toward the lift. In her room, she placed her packages on the dresser, laid her hat alongside them, and then walked into the bathroom, turning on the light. Looking into the mirror, she ran her fingers through her dark brown hair, wincing at the gray streaks starting to show.

Reaching into her purse for her comb, she ran it briskly through her rumpled, wavy hair; she reached for a washcloth, dampening it with cold water. Removing her green-framed glasses, she sighed as she felt the water's coolness on her eyelids. She reached for a towel and then turned off the light and walked to the window. She was still tired from clearing her possessions out of her office in Rabat, her plane trip to Cleveland, and the flight from Chicago, and also a bit foot-weary from the morning's shopping but pleased to be settled in London.

vi

John McKay stepped out of the first car at Lancaster Gate, the third tube stop from Oxford Circus on London's Central underground line. He rode the lift to the surface and stepped out into the West End's Bayswater section, north of Hyde Park. He looked across the street and saw he was very close to Victoria Gate, the entrance to the park near the top end of the Serpentine.

Shifting his suitcase to the other hand, he walked to Gloucester Terrace and Sussex Gardens, where the two streets connected with Bayswater Road. Walking along Gloucester Terrace, he passed a tobacconist shop and a small boutique, not really a shopping area but just a few houses in which the ground floors had been converted to businesses. He passed a small Italian restaurant, a trattoria that had a number of tables and chairs out on the sidewalk. Past Craven Road, a few of the houses had been transformed into bed-and-breakfast hotels, and toward the middle of the block stood the long terrace of Beauregard House.

In a rocking chair on the terrace, an older man sat reading a newspaper. He looked up with a faint smile and a friendly nod as John walked up the stairs. The man looked vaguely familiar to John McKay, but on second thought, he decided it was the man's smiling face, like that of a friendly salesman, that made him seem familiar. With an answering nod, he passed on through the revolving door to the lobby and stepped up to the registration desk. Standing there was Susanna Brice, smiling and looking casual but businesslike in her high-necked white blouse; she placed the phone back in its cradle and said, "Good afternoon, sir."

"Hello. My name is McKay. I have a reservation."

After searching through a file index, Susanna drew out a card. "Yes, Mr. McKay, you're expected. You'll be with us for two weeks, correct?"

At his nod, she continued, "Please sign the registration book."

He was tall, and as he bent over to sign, a lock of blondish hair curled out over his right ear. Upon signing his name and replacing the pen, he brushed his hair back with his hand, and with a half smile at Susanna, reached for the key she handed him.

"Your room is on the third floor, and the lift is over there. Will you need help?"

Shaking his head, he stepped back, reached down for his suitcase and briefcase, and turned. Straight ahead was a wide entrance leading into a lounge. He walked through the spacious lobby to the lounge to see what it was like. Looking around, he thought it wasn't exactly "Olde England" but looked comfortable. It was a long room with a number of chairs spaced around low tables in conversational groups. About halfway to the end of the room was a large television set with chairs comfortably clustered in front of it for group viewing, and at the very end of the lounge was a small bar with four bar stools. To the right of the registration desk in the lobby, there was an open area leading into a large dining room. The lifts were located in the center of the lobby's far wall. Walking back toward the reception area, he nodded to Mrs. Brice and headed for the lifts.

In his room, he put his suitcase by the chair, placed the briefcase beside it, and walked slowly around the room. He turned on the bathroom light, looked into the room, and then turned off the light and went over to the window. He stood there a few minutes, sat down on the window seat, and thought of Hannah. He should call her, but she had still been annoyed with him in her call from Birmingham last evening—still annoyed that he had accepted the training job in London and the expected project assignment in Japan that might take as long as three months. Well, the job would help his career, even if it did delay his intended marriage for a while.

vii

Down on the terrace, Charley Smith closed and folded his newspaper and thought to himself, *News from Afghanistan is bad again. More combat deaths. Funny how many wars we've had and how I just happened to miss getting into any of them—too young for the Suez Crises, a shade too old for the Vietnam War—and definitely too old to join the Vietnam war protestors. Just about too old for the Falklands War, but that was a short war anyway. Then, the Gulf War. Guess I might have been called up if that had lasted any longer. And now Afghanistan—not too old to worry about a son—if Angelina had turned out to be a boy instead.*

Getting up, he stretched and walked to the railing. His thoughts shifted. *That chap seemed too young a man to be staying at a residential hotel like this. He looked like a businessman, but if I were his age, maybe twenty-five years younger than I am now, I'd be staying at the Hilton on Park Lane or the Browne Hotel in Mayfair.*

But now, since Gwynne's passing, I really like living in this part of London. The major advertising agencies seemed to be clustered in Mayfair and Holburn, not far away, and the area was convenient to Oxford, one of the main shopping streets in the West End. It had worked out well for him that Gwynne's inventory of watercolor paintings had sold out completely during the years when her health declined.

With a grimace, he looked at his watch. *Tea time already. Well, perhaps that new guest, Mrs. Brent—Barbara—might be in the lounge.*

Chapter 2

i

Finding a strap, John McKay grabbed it as the train gave a slight lurch. *So this is Monday morning rush hour on the tube*, he thought to himself. *I'm glad it's only a few stops.*

Coming up out of the underground at the Bond Street station, he paused on the sidewalk, turning to get his bearings. He was standing on Oxford Street, and behind him, past the pub on the corner, Bond Street stretched away. He reached into his pocket for the slip of paper, took a long look at the directions again, and crossed the street as the light changed.

As he turned into Bond Street from Oxford Street, he thought he was in the wrong place. Half a block away, an elegant three-story building completely closed off the street. Puzzled, he looked at the office buildings on each side. Yes, there it was: the building painted off-white with two windows on each side of the large, ornate crimson-colored door, a polished brass plate on the wall beside it, marked in large, easy-to-read letters, "MARALLON HOUSE."

So, he thought, *the top of New Bond Street is just that—the very end of the street.* Glancing at his watch, he realized that it was a bit early, so he wandered up to look through the revolving door in the center of the building with the brass plate beside it reading "Private Club." *Not much to see here*, he thought as he retraced his steps.

Standing in front of the crimson door, he pressed the button marked "Please Ring," reached for the doorknob, and pulled the door open as the buzzer sounded.

The receptionist sitting behind her desk looked up as he walked over and said, "Good morning. My name is McKay."

He stood there with a smile on his lightly tanned face, a tall, blond young man, nicely dressed in a dark blue suit with hat in one hand, briefcase in the other. She glanced at the names on her calendar.

"To see Mr. Campbell, you're expected, Mr. McKay. Please go straight ahead to the lift, and Mr. Campbell's office is on the third floor, at the far end of the hall."

Stepping out of the lift, he could see that the door was open, and as he walked in past the people standing talking, a few looked over at him. He crossed the room to the man sitting at the large desk and held out his hand.

"Good morning, sir. I'm John McKay."

With a smile, Tim Campbell looked up, stood up, and took the outstretched hand in his firm grip. He was a tall, soldierly-looking man, his gray hair clipped close, his white mustache neatly trimmed.

"Glad to meet you, Mr. McKay. You're just in time. We're ready to start the meeting," he replied formally in a smooth Oxford accent.

In a louder voice, he said, "Ladies and gentlemen, please take a seat. This is Mr. John McKay. You'll get to meet him later. He's here on a training assignment, and you'll all get to work with him during the next few weeks."

Looking around at everyone, he continued, "For those of you who weren't here on Friday, we worked through the new product line's tentative launch schedule with Miss Madeline Claiborne here," he gestured toward her, "the expected dates for the photo sessions, a tentative series of dates for the advertising launches, and her tentative personal appearances schedule. The ad agency will supervise the photo sessions and sequence the photos into a TV storyboard for our review."

Pausing, he sat down at his desk and picked up his notes. "Now, as shown on the meeting agenda, let's start with the production schedules by product group and sell-in quantities, the sales team's sell-in story and route plans, the latest financial estimate, and so on." He turned toward Allen Black, the key product manager, who began his presentation.

Taking careful notes on his own copy of the agenda and in his notebook, John was impressed with the marketing director's smooth management control and the preparation each staff manager showed during his presentation.

As the meeting ended, Tim walked over to John and said, "I've arranged for you to have lunch with the finance director.

Come along. I'll take you to his office and introduce you. I know that he's set up some meetings for you with his staff people for this afternoon, so please come in to see me at nine o'clock tomorrow morning, and we'll go through your training program."

ii

John had missed tea that afternoon, and the Beauregard House dining room was crowded as he walked in for dinner that evening. It seemed to be mostly couples chatting and adding to the mild hum of conversation. As he sat down, he was surprised to see Madeline among the other diners, sitting at the far side of the room and reading as she appeared to be eating her dessert.

From bits of conversation during the marketing meeting, he was aware that she was from Brighton, but he'd had no idea that she was staying here. He had the urge to get up, to walk over to her, but remembered the brochure Susanna Brice had given to him with his key—the Beauregard made every attempt to preserve individual privacy, especially in the dining room. He picked up the menu, glanced at it, but looked over it to look at her again.

He had been impressed with her smiles and quick responses when she had answered questions at the meeting. Now she was more casually dressed, her streaked blond hair pinned back out of the way. As she reached for her glass, she turned slightly and at that moment reminded him of Hannah. Remembering that he wanted to talk to her, his attention turned to the phone call he had to make to Birmingham. He studied the menu this time, made his selection, passed it on to Miss Brown, the cheery young waitress, and looked at Madeline again.

She had finished her meal, closed her book, and picked up her purse, which managed to give the same impression as a briefcase. She stood up, erect, smiled at Miss Brown, and turned to leave. Glancing up, she noticed him watching her, seemed surprised, gave him a little half smile and a brief nod, moved between the other diners, and left the room.

Her survey of John seemed inconclusive, and he couldn't tell if her face had registered approval or disapproval. He had the feeling that she'd shown some of both. She was too far away for him to see the color of her eyes, but she had dark brows, a very pretty face, high cheekbones, and a perfect photographer's model nose. Her mouth gave her the impression of sternness, but it was full and broad and nicely modeled as she gave him that half smile. She looked casually fashionable, competent and businesslike, not particularly austere, but as if she might put people into handy categories.

Finishing his meal, he placed his coffee cup back in the saucer. As he reached into his coat pocket for a cigarette, he noticed the prominent "No Smoking," sign, pulled his empty hand out of his pocket, pushed back his chair, and headed for the front terrace. He rather liked the convenience of the hotel's Continental Plan, which included breakfast and dinner meals in the weekly bill.

On the terrace, as he reached for his lighter, he noticed that Madeline was sitting in a rocking chair, talking casually with that salesman-looking chap. Dropping the cigarette pack back into his pocket, he walked over toward them and leaned casually against the railing.

Looking up, she smiled her half smile and said, "Mr. Smith, this is Mr. McKay. We're both doing some work for the same company."

Extending a hand, the older man said, "I'm Charley Smith. Glad to meet you. I'm retired, and I was just saying that we don't get many younger folks here at the Beauregard. It's a refreshing change. I've been here about four months, and I really like the place. Rooms are comfortable, people are friendly, and most important, the food's good."

Charley's graying hair was beginning to thin on top, but his hardy smile showed strong white teeth as he went on to talk about opportunities he had been finding. He'd been selected to do voice-over work for TV commercials for a number of advertising agencies. It was a far cry from the sales work he had been doing for many years; but the income was always welcome, and he enjoyed the work—especially if the commercials proved to be successful in improving product sales.

"But you must excuse me—here comes Mrs. Brent. She's just arrived from America. She spent many years in the U.S. Peace Corps in Morocco, and I'd like to hear more about her experiences there."

As Charley got up and left, John sat down in the chair beside Madeline and noticed that she frowned as he started to lift his lighter to his cigarette. Sensing her displeasure, he dropped it, unlit, back into his shirt pocket and said with a grin. "I've been smoking too much lately anyway."

Even in the dim light, he saw she had bright blue eyes as he said, "I heard at the meeting this morning you were from Brighton. How long are you staying here?"

She sat motionless for a thoughtful second, her smile in place. Her very white teeth sparkled, and her features were slightly sharp but sensuous.

"I'm not sure at the moment. Marallon is looking for a particular face to launch its new cosmetics line—a thirties face that young marrieds on into their early forties can identify with—a face that could be a new mum, a young professional, or a gal wanting to return to the labor market."Pausing, she turned toward him and continued, "Not a glamorous movie star or a 'personality' like those who have recently launched whole new cosmetics lines but rather an average young woman telling a story about products that will work for her as an individual."

Breaking into a broad grin, she said, "The marketing folks think that I have the right face, but whether I stay for a month or take an early train back to Brighton is going to rest on the advertising shots taken during this week."

"That's quite a challenge—to win or lose on the success of a photographer's skill. Have you been through a situation like this before?" he asked.

"Not exactly," she said with a wry smile. "I'm a photographer's model, where the figure and clothing sizes are more important than the face. So I'm really anxious to be successful in this assignment, although my boyfriend would like it better if I were continuing to work beach modeling photo sessions in Brighton."

"Yeah, I see. I'm kind of in the same boat. I'll be tied up in London during a training program before heading off for the Far East to see whether I can help Marallon with the situation they have in Japan, but my significant other," he said wryly, "would be happy if I were working back in Birmingham."

He stood up. "I've never been to Brighton. Let's walk down to the trattoria on the next block for coffee before it gets too late, while you tell me what it's like along the seashore. We used to go to Blackpool in the summer when I was growing up."

Her shrug and laugh were self-deprecatory.

"Well, we don't have any roller coasters, but we have a pier stretching out toward France and a wide ocean rolling onto a pebble-covered beach," she said, as she rose and turned abruptly toward the stairs leading down to the street.

iii

Madeline was wearing khaki-colored slacks and a white sweater. She looked good, and to John it was clear that she had a figure that was just right for her modeling profession.

Even in the stretch pants that looked just fine on gangling teenagers, Madeline could have managed, but she looked great just as she was.

Walking along Gloucester Terrace, Madeline asked, "What's the training program you mentioned?"

"Actually, I guess 'training' isn't the right term. I'll be learning everything I can about Marallon operations here in the UK over the next several weeks."

"You mentioned going to Japan. Is it related to that?"

"Yes. My job there will be to study operations in Tokyo to make sure their procedures are the same as they are here."

"Why is that necessary?" she asked. "Wouldn't they have their own way of doing business?"

"Yes, ordinarily. But in Tokyo, three cosmetics store owners have been murdered over the past two years. They were major Marallon customers. The Tokyo police couldn't solve the crimes, and no one in the Japanese company was found to be connected with the murders."

"I see," she said. "But why are you involved?"

"The managing director of Tokyo Marallon was not satisfied. It seemed too much of a coincidence that three major customers were murdered and no motive could be found. Company operations were studied after each murder, but nothing incriminating turned up. He asked for a totally independent analysis to make sure operations in Japan were the same as those of the British parent company—in case they were doing something that was leading to the murders, which had been overlooked before."

"And Worldwide Consultants was selected."

"Right. I was working in the Worldwide office in Birmingham and was chosen, because of my background and a bit of prior time spent in Japan, to learn about Marallon operations here before heading for Tokyo."

"It's rather crowded this evening," he said as they walked up to the trattoria.

It was a pleasant evening, so most of the outside tables were taken; but they found two chairs at the table farthest from the trattoria doorway, where the hum of conversation was not too loud.

With a smile, John said, "Two cappuccinos," to the waiter as they sat down.

"Tell me. What's it like living in Brighton?"

Placing her purse on her lap, Madeline replied, "I guess it's different being raised there from childhood rather than just taking the family for a tourist vacation. Generally, the tourists rent rooms at one of the B&Bs for a week, lounge on the beach, or take the kids for long walks along the surf looking for shells."

Pausing, she continued, "They usually visit the Royal Pavilion and spend some time on the pier. In my case, I did those things too, but I attended school there through the sixth form then went on to the University of Exeter in the West Country."

"What did you do then?" he asked.

Speaking slowly, she said, "When I graduated, I was offered a job by a modeling agency in Brighton. I felt I couldn't refuse. It seemed like such a great opportunity."

"Sounds promising," he said with a grin as the coffee arrived.

She brushed back her hair. "It was fun modeling expensive clothes, but most of the assignments were oriented toward the beach, posing in swimsuits with new car models—and even in furniture ads."

Reaching for her coffee cup, she continued, "It's been an interesting career, but my grandmother convinced me that I could do a lot better in a business career. So this cosmetics launch, with my face in national advertising and PR interviews, is the first step, I hope, toward relaunching my own personal career—provided I make it through the first photo sessions."

They went on talking about possible career opportunities that she might look into, about her upcoming photo sessions, the launch campaign for Marallon's new product line, and about travel opportunities for her as she moved to different locations around England for her promotional demonstrations.

Finally, she straightened, leaned back in her chair, signaled the waiter for a half-cup refill, and turned to look at John.

"But you're not involved with the launch campaign; in fact, you don't look like you should even be connected with a cosmetics company."

With a wry smile, he hunched his shoulders and ran his right hand over his nose. "Yeah, I know what you mean. My nose got a little bent during my freshman year on the Birmingham University rugby team, and now, even though I'm a big guy, I've got to favor the right leg just a bit when the weather's rainy."

Then, speaking thoughtfully, he said, "It's possible to think about the operations analysis that I'm doing here at Marallon to be a rather low-key consulting engagement, but the situation in Tokyo is focused on murder and whether there's a management problem allowing or encouraging it to happen. It doesn't matter whether it's a cosmetics company, a steel company, or a shoe company, the focus is on the people, the processes, and the operational conditions. The same applies whether the company is located here, in Scotland, or in Japan."

Dropping his napkin beside his coffee cup, he said, "I'm anxious to get started on this program, and I've still got to review the final report on my last assignment in York; so if you've finished we can start back."

She took a gaudy head scarf out of her purse and pulled it over her hair, pushed her big sunglasses back in, stood up, and stepped away from the table as he handed some money to the waiter.

iv

Pierre and Nicole's trip from Haywards Heath to Paddington had been short, and their conversation was filled with Nicole's recollections of her two-week stay with her sister, Michelle, and her family. Usually Nicole was a quiet, self-assured person, her graying hair curly around her ears and almost down to her collar; but it had been a long time since her last visit, and it had been a busy two weeks.

Back at the hotel, on the sidewalk turning up onto the broad stairs leading to the Beauregard Terrace, Pierre Duval turned to Nicole and said, "Let's go right into the dining room. I think there's still enough time to finish dinner before they close the doors."

"Alright," she said. "You take the luggage up to the room. I can make a rest stop just off the lobby and will go right in to our table."

Pierre headed for the lift, dropped off the luggage, and then joined Nicole at the table.

"Nice to see you back, Mr. Duval," said Miss Brown as she handed him a menu. "Hope you had a pleasant trip."

With a smile and a thank you, Pierre turned, nodded to the couple at the next table, and began to study the menu. He glanced at it somewhat absentmindedly; he was still concerned about the conversation he'd had with Wentz on the train ride from Newhaven. Isaac Wentz had met him there when he arrived on the ferry from Dieppe.

"Well," Nicole asked, "what looks good?"

"Haven't quite decided," he answered with a shrug, but with Miss Brown standing there, they both made hurried selections.

He waited until they were finishing their dessert.

"I'm going to go down to Dorchester for a few days," he said as he wiped his lips and placed the napkin beside his plate. She looked up, surprised for a moment, but then he went on to tell her that Wentz had been "damned mysterious."

"He told me his contact is interested in nuclear risk assessment and research on the subject offers rich rewards. He didn't offer any more information than that, but he was sure my reputation as a researcher in radiological physics was of interest. He offered two hundred pounds if I'd ride down to Dorchester in Dorset for consultation, or an interview, I think."

He leaned over toward her and said, "I'm really hesitant about going. Wentz's contact is from a Middle Eastern country. I'm not sure that 'contact' is the right word for his relationship with this friend of his. According to what I've heard, Wentz was lured away from the Department of Energy under very curious circumstances after I left the Department. I really didn't know him very well when we worked there."

Pausing to finish his last bit of coffee, he continued, "Now weapons of mass destruction are suspected in Iraq, and Iran is having political disputes with us and other countries over its nuclear program. I don't want to get involved with a possible terrorist state—especially now with the war going on in Afghanistan."

Pierre noticed that Miss Brown was hovering near their table, and it was clear that almost all of the other diners had left.

Pushing his chair back, he got up and took Nicole's hand as she walked around the table.

"I told him that I was fully engaged in a research project now, and I wouldn't take on anything considered a conflict of interest. Of course, between you and me, if the research field was interesting and it resulted in a well-paying position for a few years, I'd like to talk about it. Anyway, since he agreed to that, I told him I'd make the trip." Duval's lips parted in a grin.

"Well, for a retiree, two hundred pounds for the maximum of a three-day excursion to Dorset sounds pretty good." Nodding to another couple, they walked through the lobby and out onto the terrace.

Just then, John and Madeline, returning from the trattoria, started up the steps to the terrace from the sidewalk. Seeing Pierre and Nicole standing there, Madeline stopped, looked sharply at Pierre, and said, "What a coincidence. Didn't we ride in the same train carriage from Brighton two days ago?"

Looking at her intently, he replied, "Why, yes we did. But actually, I was coming from the Dieppe ferry stop at Newhaven."

Nodding, she said with a smile, "I thought you looked French at the time."

Smiling, he turned to look at Nicole. "No. We're both American now. We live in Washington."

Extending his hand, he said, "My name's Pierre, and this is my wife, Nicole."

"I'm Madeline, and this is my friend, John," she said as they all shook hands.

Turning toward Nicole, Madeline asked, "How long will you be staying?"

"Looks like we'll be headed home in about a week won't we?" she replied as she looked up at her husband.

Smiling, Madeline said, "I hope we can chat a bit before you leave." as they went on into the lounge.

Pierre turned, looking for chairs on the terrace. Most were occupied, but they found two together and sat down not far from Charley Smith, who was sitting talking to Mrs. Brent.

V

Their chairs had been pulled fairly close together, and Charley, in his persuasive voice-over baritone, was speaking.

"Last time we chatted, you mentioned that you had just arrived from Rabat after many years with the American Peace Corps, so if you don't mind, I'd like to hear more about Morocco."

"Actually, I arrived from Cleveland—had gone there to spend a few weeks with relatives. I lived there for a few years before I joined the Peace Corps."

"How did you happen to join up, and why Morocco? Did you enjoy living in that country?"

"I've always been interested in social work. Mother and Dad were very active in church work when I was growing up. As far as North Africa is concerned, it just so happened that I was offered a position there."

"I see. My wife and I had different kinds of interests. I was in sales for many years, and my wife was a very talented watercolor artist. We traveled quite a bit to give her a chance to paint various kinds of architecture, but we never traveled to North Africa."

Barbara sensed that he was speaking too loudly. Feeling a need for privacy and not wanting to be overheard in matters so personal, she moved over a bit in her chair, took a sip from her glass, and turned to face him.

She appeared far too young to be retired, her face bearing only a few smile lines; the color of her dark eyes almost matched her curly hair, which was graying slightly and was piled on top of her head. In quiet phrases and fragments, occasional sighs, and beautifully timed hesitations, she painted the flavor of influence in President Kennedy's original appeal for volunteers many years ago.

"Morocco was among the first to invite the Peace Corps to assist in economic development and manpower needs. After my preassignment schooling in the U.S., I reported to the country director of the Peace Corps in the U.S. Embassy at Rabat."

She talked of the first group of English language teachers to arrive, the various sites and locations, the need for water development, about her own working in Rabat, and then her assignment to Meknes.

"I must admit that we all felt considerably uneasy during the first weeks following the 9/11 attack on the U.S. by Muslim terrorists. In fact, that's the basic reason I chose to retire at this time. While it seems that terrorists could strike America again, and there's no evidence of threats against foreigners in Morocco, I felt vulnerable living in a Muslim country."

In the gathering twilight, traffic in the neighborhood had all but ended; the hum of conversation along the long veranda had quieted as occasional laughter trailed off and other guests left.

She straightened, sighed. "Well, Charley, that's enough for one evening. Let's step to the TV in the lounge and see if we can catch the evening news."

She stood up, put her hand to her lips to stifle a yawn, and stepped toward the railing. She took a deep breath of the cool evening air and turned to Charley with a smile.

"Next time, it's your turn to tell me more about your world," she said as they walked into the lobby and turned left toward the lounge.

One couple was sitting toward the center of the room by the television, and Colonel Johnson was sitting by a lamp not far from the door reading a newspaper.

Charley stopped and said, "Barbara, this is a longtime resident. I'd like to introduce you to Colonel Glenn Johnson, British Army, retired."

Hearing his name mentioned, the Colonel pushed his reading glasses up onto his forehead and looked up. He cleared his throat with a *hmmph* and stood up holding his paper in his left hand.

With a smile, Charley said, "Colonel, this is Mrs. Barbara Brent, newly arrived from America after an exciting career with the U.S. Peace Corps in Morocco." Smiling broadly, the Colonel looked admiringly at the young-looking face and dark hair. She was almost as tall as he was and looked particularly nice in her yellow sweater, white slacks, and jade necklace.

"Nice to meet you, Mrs. Brent," he said in his clipped British Army voice as he extended his hand.

"Perhaps we can swap tales about Morocco. I was a young major stationed in our embassy in Rabat for a short time, following the first Gulf War, but perhaps that was before your arrival there."

"Well, it wasn't," she said with a smile as she shook his hand, "but I doubt if much has changed over the years. I'd be pleased to talk about the country and the people I met there. Nice to meet you, Colonel."

Turning to Charley, she said, "Thank you for introducing me. Now, let's see if we can catch the evening news."

Chapter 3

i

The next morning after breakfast, Pierre, standing in the lobby with a small suitcase and briefcase in hand, leaned over, gave Nicole a tender kiss, and told her he'd call when he'd gotten settled in Dorchester. Then he pushed his way through the revolving door and headed for Waterloo Station.

Riding in a first-class carriage, he had plenty of time to sort through a few notes from his briefcase since Salisbury would be his first stop. It was a bother to have to change trains, and it again made him wonder, *Why Dorchester?* It was such a small, out-of-the-way place in the southwest; nothing connected with nuclear research was located in the vicinity. It wasn't even a resort center, so why would anyone be staying there? The closest such activity was at the Culham Science Centre in Oxfordshire, but that really wasn't very close. At least Isaac Wentz would be meeting him at the station.

ii

At Beauregard House two hours before, at 6:00 AM, John had pushed through the revolving door and stepped out onto the terrace. His sweat suit felt just about right for the early morning temperature as he started a very slow jog down Gloucester Terrace and headed for Hyde Park. The trattoria tables had been pulled back against the wall, and a long security cable threaded through the chairs.

It was cool and pleasant, and the traffic along Bayswater was beginning to pick up as he slowed down to wait for the light. He was glad to be back in his running shoes again. It had been over a week since he had been jogging along the beach road at Ramsgate, and there wasn't much certainty that his intensive program would let him spend much time running in the park.

Across the street, through Victoria Gate, past the fountains, and toward the Peter Pan statue, he thought about Hannah as he jogged. Too bad she was still fretting about his stay in London. Her job at the stock brokerage office was causing anxiety, as the market moves didn't seem to be any less volatile now that second-quarter earnings statements were being released. She missed the many quiet evenings they'd had together, talking about market-related situations and her portfolio, which had been doing well.

When he had graduated with his master's degree, she had liked the idea of his joining Worldwide Consultants rather than beginning work in the foreign exchange department of the Midland bank, which had offered him a starting position. For the first few years, the local consulting engagements in and around Birmingham had gone well, but the idea of longer projects that might take him away from the city, even out of the country for extended periods, became an irritation to her. She missed him and liked the idea of his being close by.

He, on the other hand, had liked the idea of working on a variety of management problems in different kinds of companies and was impressed with the caliber of the specialists he was working with at Worldwide. He liked their conservative thinking and their interest in the policies of the Conservative Party in Parliament. In a way, he had been lucky in not having a strong academic background in a particular specialty like finance or marketing. Worldwide's Birmingham management had been willing to let him tackle problems with a broader view that stretched across major business functions rather than focusing on specific, detailed problems. He particularly liked the idea of developing proposals and making bids offering Worldwide's services to major firms in the Midlands.

He passed the statue, and his thoughts turned to Madeline. It had been a long evening for both of them. But it had been longer for Madeline. As they were walking back to Beauregard House last evening, she had tried to avoid talking about some personal problems.

She had hesitated before answering quietly, when he'd asked whether she'd had any particular problems while modeling. Her *no* was hesitant. "Except for the amorous photographers and agency guys who seemed to think that the models owed them some special favors in return for using their bodies in their ad campaigns," she had explained.

"It was the real professionals in the field, who didn't try to feel the 'merchandise' under the clothes that made it a pleasure to work in photography," she said.

And her reply to his question about whether there was a particular young man in her life was even more hesitant. It was a definite yes, but she said it in a way that seemed to say that the feeling was stronger on his side than on hers.

"Wendell has been such a great help to me during a very difficult time. I know he loves me, and I'm very fond of him. He wants me to marry him, but I feel that I've got to move ahead in what I want to do in my career. He's a successful agent for a prominent insurance company in Brighton, but I don't feel ready to settle down and start a family right now. I think he understands, but he seems so impatient at times."

John appreciated her honesty and her deeply felt need to make better use of her college training, to progress toward more specific business objectives, to set a goal and reach it.

He said, "Far too many young people today seem to have no driving need to reach any particular objective. If it feels good, do it! That's their only consideration."

The cry of the Beat Generation was not his idea of worthwhile living in today's changing world—or hers either.

John slowed to a walk, breathing heavily as he reached the end of the lake where the sidewalk joined Rotten Row. His right knee was just beginning to feel the strain. Time to walk back on the other side of the Serpentine.

As he rounded the end of the lake, his thoughts turned to his meeting with Tim and the details of his training program. The major unknowns were the specific people he'd be working with and the timing, since the new launch program had not been revealed during early discussions about the project in Tokyo.

He thought about the training program in relation to the situation that the company was facing in Japan. The murders of the store owners had not been solved, and there were no clues tying the crimes to Marallon; so the training program was designed to give him a broad overview of each of the UK company's business functions.

Whether this would be adequate to give him enough background to come up with a solid course for analysis was still not clear—and wouldn't be evident until he got to Tokyo.

His thoughts turned again to his previous experience in Japan. He had been fortunate as a very young officer to be assigned to the British Embassy in Tokyo concerned with British government matters in the Far East. The physical training that was a part of his service had not been as strenuous as it would have been in the enlisted ranks, so the weakness in his knee hadn't become a problem.

The assignment hadn't lasted very long before he was demobbed, released to civilian life and his graduate classes in Birmingham, but he felt that it had been long enough for him to gain a basic understanding of the Japanese and their culture. He felt confident that he could deal with Marallon's situation in Tokyo.

Unfortunately, the language barrier was almost impenetrable, and many streets in Tokyo didn't have signs—even in Japanese, let alone English. With Japan's combination of breathtaking scenery, vibrant cities, great food, and unique culture, one would think that there would be more English-speaking people doing business there. Fortunately, Marallon was able to attract sufficient English-speaking translators and interpreters, so working there would probably not be too difficult. But he wondered whether he could count on really accurate translation when questionable processes or situations arose. That was certainly one more problem he had to think about.

Walking back through Victoria Gate, John crossed Bayswater Road, jogged slowly along Gloucester Terrace, and turned up onto the steps at the Beauregard. He moved through the revolving door on his way to a shower and a cooked English breakfast.

iii

Madeline, sitting at her regular table by the windows at the far side of the dining room, was finishing the Fashion column in the *Morning Star* as she pushed her plate back and reached for her coffee cup. She had never read the *Star* in Brighton and was surprised at how much sex and celebrity stuff filled its pages. There didn't seem to be any world news at all, and she wasn't really interested in who was seeing who in what "Hot Spots." Laying the paper aside, she signaled Betty for a second cup, leaned back in her chair, and thought about her trip to the agency's office in Chelsea. It was a nice neighborhood, and she liked the few people that she'd met during her first visit.

The photographer who had made the first set of proof shots with the mock-ups of the new cosmetic line had been very professional. She liked that but was still somewhat nervously looking forward to the day's photo sessions. Based on her past experience, she felt the results would be really outstanding, and she was beginning to think of the launch schedule and her personal appearances.

Well, one thing at a time, she cautioned herself. *Now it's time to get moving.* She glanced around the room, nodded to a couple at the next table, and moved toward the door. She thought she might see John, and her eyes swept the room in search of him; but he wasn't there.

With a smile, she greeted Susanna Brice at the doorway and then moved through the lobby. Glancing at the phone booths, she thought about calling Wendell this evening and pushed through the revolving door on her way to the underground.

Coming up out of the tube stop at Sloane Square, she walked down King's Road a few blocks and turned onto Sloane Avenue. It had been a month since she had been there, but she easily found the agency's office.

The door latch buzzed when she pressed the button marked "Please Ring," and she stepped into the fantasy of the advertising world where the skills of artists, copywriters, editors, TV technicians, and photographers combined to transform ordinary jars of something or other into some of the most wanted products on housewives' shopping lists. The skills of the scientists and chemists were in competition with those of the wordsmiths to see who could best formulate and sell products and who could best describe them in such a way that they were bought, used, and admired by the vast majority of young women, and treasured by those making every attempt to age gracefully.

"Good morning. I'm Madeline Claiborne. I'm here to start work on the new Marallon cosmetics products advertising campaign," she said with a smile to the receptionist.

"Of course. Please come this way. The account executive, Mrs. Hastings, is expecting you."

They went up the stairs, down a long hallway, and past a few offices, finally stopping to knock on a door at the end of the corridor. It was opened by a tall, dark-haired, attractive woman not much older than Madeline who led them into a large, well-lighted office crowded with tables on which jars and bottles of cosmetic products were stacked and piled in various displays.

"Good morning. I'm Louisa Hastings. I know you're Madeline. I've seen the proof photos taken during your first visit," she said with a smile.

"I was out of town at the time. I'm sorry I missed meeting you. Please sit down." she said as the receptionist turned and left the office.

Louisa continued, "I've been looking through your portfolio. You have an impressive background. I'm happy to be working with you."

As she raised her head, her well-made-up skin looked almost flawless in the light from the window. Her short hair was jet black and looked squeaky clean; her eyes were almost as dark as her hair, and the pearl earrings she wore perfectly matched the set of choker pearls lying up close to her throat over her black knit sweater.

Hesitating, Madeline said, "I'm from Brighton—and I know that London accents are different—but you don't sound like you're from London."

"No," Louisa replied with a laugh. "I was born in Johannesburg, South Africa. My dad was an electrical engineer with Eskom, South Africa's electric utilities company for many years."

"My, that's interesting. How did you get here?" Madeline asked.

"I completed my studies in the private school system and went on to the University of Witwatersrand where I majored in public relations and advertising. I came here when we all emigrated a few years ago."

Moving away from her desk, Louisa continued, "But, let me show you Marallon's new skin care group. It will be launched as part of the new product line. Production samples just came from the factory in Brentford. Over here," she said as she walked over to one of the tables and proceeded to discuss various cleansers, toners, and revitalizing lotions.

They heard a knock on the open door as Tom Lambert, the agency's senior photographer, walked in. He strode toward Madeline with his hand outstretched.

"Hello there, Madeline. Nice to see you again. Sorry to break in, Louisa, but I'm all set to begin work in the studio."

Madeline thought, *Anyone would know immediately he was a photographer just by looking at him.* He looked like a professional, was about average size with white hair and white Abe Lincoln whiskers, but his eyes seemed to be sizing everybody up for his next photo.

"Come on, let's get started," he said as he reached for Madeline's arm, smiled at Louisa, and moved toward the door.

The studio and dressing room were on the third floor, and the bright morning sun was flooding through the slanted skylight windows. Louisa had followed them up the stairs with the draft storyboards under her arm and the scripts in her briefcase. Jimmy,

Tom's assistant, and the sound engineers were waiting for them, so after a costume change for Madeline, they were off to a full morning of productive work.

iv

John came out of the Bond Street underground entrance, crossed Oxford, and rang the bell at Marallon's crimson door. After a stop at the reception desk and a short ride in the lift, he knocked on the marketing director's open door.

"Come in, John. Have a chair," Tim said as he reached for a folder in his desk drawer.

"I'm having a sales meeting here shortly, so after we go over your training schedule, I'd like you to stay for the meeting," he said, handing John the folder.

"Here's a list of the people you'll be working with, along with their offices and phone numbers, and a proposed timetable for the next two weeks. There are a few minor changes from the schedule discussed with you at Ramsgate, but they're due to the new product launch. Please look it over and come back to me if you have any questions."

Looking down at a copy of the list on his desk, he continued, "You'll notice Ireland has been added to your schedule. You'll be working with Brian Donovan, our general manager in Dublin. We added it because Ireland, its people, and its government have positioned themselves at the high end of the business of life science, including pharmaceuticals and related industries. We'll be talking about this again since Japan is taking the same approach. We're looking for new ideas to come from biotech research."

Leafing through the personnel folder, Tim looked up and said, "I'm glad to see your background is in management and not necessarily in auditing or accounting, although they may become very important during your work in Japan. Being able to take a seasoned overview may be your most important skill." He paused.

"That's why we chose Worldwide. Like major publicly owned companies, Marallon has used a variety of accountancy firms over the years, and we still use one of the Big Four to do the company auditing. We've used the same firm for a number of years, but we agreed with the managing director in Tokyo that under the present circumstances it would be better to use an outside consultant firm to review their operating procedures there."

Upon hearing a knock on the open door, Tim looked up and gestured for the staff member to enter. He said, "John, you remember Mike Ryan; you've met him before. He's our sales manager, responsible for the sell-in campaign. You'll be calling on a few key accounts with Mike in the London area, and he'll go into more detail with you after this meeting. But here are the other key players in the launch, so someone please shut the door. Let's get started."

V

At the advertising agency, the photo sessions went very well, and at one o'clock, when they broke for lunch, Louisa Hastings invited Madeline to join her.

"Let's walk around the corner to Sloane Square. We can have a fast sandwich and check out the latest fashions with a little window shopping."

"Fine. And that will give me a chance to talk to you about the personal appearances," said Madeline as she reached into her bag for her sunglasses.

As they walked down the last few steps to the ground floor, Louisa said, "I want to check in with a colleague. I'll meet you at the front door."

Madeline idly looked at the samples of advertisements prepared by the agency, which were mounted on the walls of the reception area. She had known what she wanted when she first went into modeling. But now, here among professional women, she realized she'd been content to just drift along. *Yes, that's just what I've been doing. Drifting through life.* She felt that she was no longer the clearheaded, resolute girl who had left Exeter. Her intelligence had been directed into specialized, well-defined fashion channels. But the fashion world continued to design for youth and was constantly moving toward younger fashions.

Thinking of the future, Madeline's thoughts slipped from the world of fashion to the immediately personal—herself and Wendell. That was the problem, the real problem. *Do I really want to marry Wendell? Settle down in an apartment in Hove, begin having children, become a stay-at-home mum?*

Louisa walked over to her. " Ready?" Smiling, chatting, they went down the front steps and turned onto King's Road.

Madeline was quiet for a few moments and then said to Louisa, "I'm hoping that my appearances really help to build Marallon product sales, but at the same time I hope I'm successful in developing ways to promote myself. I have the educational background, and I'm most anxious to find a career path that will get me away from my modeling career and started into a meaningful position in business."

With a nod, Louisa replied, "Yes, I can see how you might feel that way. Well, we'll have lots of opportunities during the launch and the follow-on personal appearances to talk about career choices in the business world and to focus your interests on specific kinds of professions."

Stopping in front of a restaurant, Louisa looked in the large front window and said, "I'm feeling a bit peckish—had early breakfast. I like this place. They serve great sandwiches, and it looks like we missed the busiest part of the lunch crowd. Look OK to you?" Getting an answering nod from Madeline, she led the way into Maryanne's Tearoom.

Chapter 4

i

The train was slowing for its stop in Dorchester. Pierre Duval shuffled a few papers back into his briefcase and slipped into his jacket. The compartment hadn't been crowded. Most of the morning commuter traffic went the other way, toward London.

He was still wondering why this meeting was being held in Dorchester. The closest UK Atomic Energy Authority was at the Winfrith site here in Dorset, but that former civil nuclear research installation was on a fast track to restoration. Public news releases had stated that UKAEA had completed over a third of the clean-up program and was set to become the first major nuclear site to be fully decommissioned, so that couldn't possibly be the reason for holding the meeting in Dorchester. Besides, the decommissioning didn't have anything to do with his area of expertise.

He wished Wentz had been more specific during their short ride on the train from Newhaven. *Well, let's see what this is all about*, he thought. With his briefcase and small suitcase in hand, he stepped down the train steps and walked along the train platform.

He found Isaac Wentz standing near the waiting room. Wentz held out his hand, and Pierre walked up to him with a broad smile.

"Glad to see you, Isaac," he said as they shook hands.

Isaac smiled. "Good morning, Pierre. I have a car in the parking lot, but let's have a fast cup of coffee in the coffee shop here. We have a meeting scheduled a short drive from here, so we'll be there in time for lunch. I'll drop you off at the hotel after our afternoon meeting."

"OK. There's room over there by the windows." After giving their order to a waiter, they took seats at a table.

"Well, Isaac, we didn't have time to chat on our short train ride. It's been over a year since our days at DOE. Where did you go when you left the agency? What have you been doing? How long have you been in England? How did you happen to find me in Newhaven?"

"It seems like a long story, Pierre, but it really hasn't been that long since you retired. Not long after you left, I was offered a job I couldn't refuse—the money was too good," Isaac said.

"I found myself in a strange situation. I'm Jewish, as you know, but I was recruited by representatives from a Middle Eastern country—I wasn't sure which one. With the war going on in Afghanistan, at first, I was really afraid to even think of accepting the job offer. But they had connections with the National Institute of Nuclear Physics in Torino, Italy. Within a few short weeks, I was working there as a researcher in one of their studies of the fundamental components of matter, in the field of subnuclear physics." He paused for a moment as the waiter came by with their coffee.

He continued, "Then, last week, during a visit visit to the European Organization for Nuclear Research, I ran into a few people that I'd met at international conferences, and one of them, Terry Hopkins, knew that you were at a meeting in France."

Taking a sip from his cup, he said, "Then, back in Torino, it so happened they were looking for research candidates, but the jobs were not for work in Italy. I thought of you and told them a bit about your background. They were interested, so a phone call back to CERN gave me all I needed to know about when the meeting in Dieppe was ending. I was asked to fly in from Torino and meet you. I had no idea where you were staying in France. Hopkins knew that you were returning to England, so I was able to find the ferry schedule and meet you in Newhaven. You're very well known in our profession, so it really wasn't that hard to find you."

He reached for the coffeepot that the waiter had left and poured himself another cup, motioning to Pierre, who shook his head. Pierre sat back in his chair and reached for his cup.

"Well, Isaac, I didn't realize that I was so easy to find, but I've been puzzled as to why we're here in Dorchester. Why here? It certainly seems to be an out-of-the-way location for anything connected with nuclear instrumentation and methods in physics research."

"You're right, but to the west, on the way toward Bridgeport, there's a wide spot in the road that has a golf course, three hotels, some expensive modern villas on the edge of the golf course, a row of what were expensive shops before the first Gulf War, but no train station. My contact lives very, very quietly in one of those villas. So if you're ready, let's be on our way."

ii

John McKay was feeling a bit weary as he pushed through the revolving door at Beauregard House. Sliding out of his jacket, he walked over to Susanna Brice, who was sitting at the reception desk.

"Hi," he said, "I'm going to be working here in the London area for the next two weeks, then expect to be away the following two weeks. I see that the hotel is very popular and quite busy, so I hope that you'll have room for me when I return."

Reaching for the registration register, she flipped through the pages, then paused and replied, "It doesn't look like that will be a problem. I'm not sure you'll have the same room, but I'll try to have it open."

"Good," he said. "I like it here. It's very convenient and very comfortable." He picked up his briefcase and headed toward the lift.

The elevator door opened, and Madeline stepped out. She stopped and smiled. "How was your day?" she asked.

"Fine," he replied. "Can I tell you about it over dinner? I'll be right down."

As he stepped into the elevator, she said, "OK, I'll be at my regular table near the window."

She nodded to a couple seated near the doorway and waved good evening to Colonel Johnson, who was seated nearby with Barbara Bates. When she reached her table, she pulled out a chair and sat down.

She picked up the menu, opened it, and looked at it—but she really didn't see it. Her thoughts turned to the day's events. The morning's product shots had gone easily. There had been a lot of them, but the first proofs had looked great; so she felt more secure about her role in the launch.

The afternoon's work with the storyboards had gone well too. Remarkably, there had been few retakes. And she felt very comfortable chatting with Louisa. She was a very friendly person and seemed to want to help Madeline in her search for the right steps to take toward a career in business.

Her eyes finally focused on the menu, but images of Wendell seemed to flood her thoughts. He had been very helpful; after all, people don't like a coroner's inquest (even if the coroner did acquit her of all blame). She had been congratulated on her courage and presence of mind, she remembered. The inquest could not have gone any better. Even Mrs. Johnson had been very kind to her. *Only Wendell ...* But she couldn't think of Wendell.

With a sigh, she turned her thoughts back to the menu, and she had already ordered when John sat down at the table.

" Well, what looks good this evening?" he asked with a smile.

"The ravioli and a salad sounded good to me," she said as she reached for her napkin.

"I didn't have time for tea this afternoon." He had changed into a sport shirt, and the dark blue color seemed to lighten the blue of his eyes. She liked what she saw.

"Sounds good to me too," he said to Miss Brown as he handed her his menu.

Turning to Madeline, he said, "So, you had a good day. What was the agency like?"

As she quietly ran through the day's events, he couldn't help but watch her. She was such a pretty woman; she smiled a lot and spoke very clearly and with a broad choice of words. Her hair was pushed back again, but the shine from the small chandelier highlighted the blondness of her hair close to her forehead.

Their meals arrived, and as he reached for his fork, John said, "Sounds like your day was a success. And Louisa Hastings seems like a good gal to have as a friend. But enough about business. You've told me about the pier, the beach scene, and the pavilion at Brighton, but you didn't mention your home life. Do you have any brothers or sisters?" he asked.

Then, against the very low hum of other conversations in the room, in the soft glow of the overhead light, she started to talk about herself, speaking in a contented and confident-sounding voice.

He liked listening to her. At first, he heard only the sound of her voice, not the meaning of her words, but then he caught the sense of the story she was telling.

"Yes, my brother Jack is three years younger than I am, so I had my share of babysitting when we were young."

She went on, talking at length about growing up in Brighton, trips to museums with her parents, springtime swimming at the beach, visits to relative's homes, early days coping with her first bicycle.

"What business is your dad in?"

"He's a local politician, so we had what I'd call a strict upbringing, avoiding anything that would reflect badly on dad's image as a trustworthy representative of the people. He's a member of the Conservative Party, so it's been a struggle since Labor won the majority of seats in Parliament."

"You went to school in Brighton?"

"Yes, and it was a bit rough in school." She talked on about the early years, learning elementary French, having trouble with math, having fun as a teenager.

"In the sixth form," she said, "we had school dances, but my parents always strictly enforced the 'get home early after the dance' rule."

"Did you play any sports?"

"Yes, I was a member of the archery team and was pretty much a tomboy, so I didn't have many boyfriends while I was growing up."

She had been eating slowly while talking. The waitress finally picked up their plates and brought their desserts, and Madeline resumed.

"Actually, my grandmother, my father's mother, had the strongest influence on my life. Her strong Conservative views led my dad into politics after he graduated from law school.

And I have fond memories of her frequent visits to our home in Brighton. She now lives in Cambridge where she retired after Grandfather Claiborne was killed."

She paused, reached for her cup, sipping at the last bit of cold coffee, and then looked at him.

He smiled and said, "It's early yet, and there's plenty of light on these long summer evenings. Let's go for a walk in the park."

As they walked down the front stairs of the hotel and along Gloucester Terrace, he started telling her about his day, his meetings for the rest of the week with the London office management staff, and that he'd be traveling with Mike Ryan, the sales manager, making calls on key accounts in the London area.

As they passed the trattoria, she said, "Didn't you say that you're from Birmingham?"

"Yes."

"Oh, I've never been there. What's it like?"

He hesitated a moment, then admitted," Well, I'm not really from Birmingham. I say that because everyone knows where it is."

They crossed Bayswater, passed through Victoria Gate, and followed the walk along the Serpentine. A faint breeze rippled the water of the lake, and other walkers seemed to be moving slowly too.

He went on, "It's a big city with a population over one million, 'the workshop of the world'. It's dynamic, moving ahead in today's world, and I like the idea of being part of it, of being thought of as a Brummie, although I don't have a Brummie accent."

"Brighton's a small town compared with that," she said.

Speaking quietly and rather slowly in the lengthening shadows of the shaded walk, he continued.

"Actually, I was raised in the nearby town of Stourbridge. I guess you could call it a western suburb of the city. It's been there since the year 1200 or longer. We lived on Pedmore, a very old street. It was narrow, lined with sprawling Victorian houses, sitting tall and narrow."

"Sounds beautiful."

"Our house had—and still has—iron fences and two metal deer under the elm trees on the front lawn."

He stopped speaking. She didn't say anything, but he felt the closeness of the silence between them grow. The gentle breeze lifted the faint fragrance of her perfume. Light and flowery with a hint of heavier musk, it suited her.

"What business is your father in?" she asked.

"Dad's a manager in a glass manufacturing firm. He inherited his interest in glass from my mother's side of the family, which had been in the town for decades. He moved up fairly quickly in sales and became an important member of the Glass Association."

"Did you ever feel you wanted to go into the glass industry?"

"Not exactly. Dad was an apprentice in the basics of the business, blowing and cutting. I never had that kind of experience."

Quietly, almost without thinking, he continued. "I suppose I should feel more affinity with the historic part of my heritage, the art of fine glass, but I'm torn between that and my attachment to the big city."

"Did you go to school in the big city?"

"Yeah. I received my graduate degree from the university there, and it's now more a part of me than my small-town upbringing."

"Well, I guess that makes us both small-town people," she said jokingly, "both trying to make our way in the city."

They had crossed the Serpentine, walking along the roadway that bisected the lake, and had returned along the walk on the other side. They sat down on the low wall by the fountains, chatting idly about little things that had happened during the day, the residents at the Beauregard, the large number of ducks along the lakeshore.

"It's been a pleasant evening," he said. "I'm not sure I'll have time for many more like this."

She looked over, curious, and said, "Oh?"

"Mike Ryan was telling me how difficult it is getting to see key accounts here during the day. The sales department is setting up the product line in Marallon House and inviting major buyers in to place orders. Some buyers can't get there during the workday and come in after closing, so that means evening hours at the office. Many won't come in at all, so we go to those accounts, which are mostly away from the center of the city. It means we might not get back to the office until eight o'clock or later."

"Sounds like long working days."

"Yes, and that will be going on in sales territories all over the UK, but I'm just sampling the sales program here in London. Equally important will be three full days working at the production, warehousing, and shipping facility at Brentford. And then on the following Sunday, I leave for a week in Scotland and Wales, and later to Ireland to see a small self-contained production and marketing operation like what the Japanese company has in Kyoto."

"I see," she nodded. Looking at her watch, she said, "It's getting late, but let's stop at the trattoria on the way back."

There were a few empty tables when they walked in. With a broad smile and a hearty *Good evening*, the waiter with the strong Italian accent took their order for two chocolate ice creams.

Dropping her purse into her lap, Madeline looked up and said, "John, I have an idea. I was planning to ride the train to Cambridge on Saturday to visit my grandmother, but since you're going to be busy for the next two weeks, why don't I just rent a car and you can come with me."

"Great idea!" He smiled.

Reaching for a napkin, she continued, "I'd love to have you meet her, and we'll be back at the Beauregard before dark so that you'll have time to get organized a bit for the busy time ahead."

"Gram's not very tall—shorter than I am. Her hair is almost completely white, and she wears black a good deal of the time. She has a wonderful smile and a very warm heart."

Smiling broadly, she said, "I should warn you she's very conservative and very much politically oriented. She really hated to see Tony Blair win the last election, but she's very practical and recognizes that nothing stays the same—everything changes. She rolls with the punches and stays up with the latest trends. I think you'll like her," she said as the bowls of ice cream arrived, and she reached for a spoon.

"Wonderful," he said. "Thank you for suggesting it. Time is flying very quickly. You should be finished at the agency next week, and the factory will start shipping to key accounts as soon as orders are released. Advertising spots should start to break while I'm still here in London, and your early promotions should be going ahead during the next few weeks. It's a good time to have a day together while we can. It seems to me that we have lots in common—seem to have had similar early lives and appear to be focusing on similar goals for the years ahead. Agree?"

"Yes, I do, John. And I'm looking forward to the trip. I'll ask Mrs. Brice to reserve a car for me at the airport. We can take the bus to Heathrow early Saturday morning, pick up the car, ride the M25 north, get on the M11 motorway, and be in Cambridge in time for lunch with Gram—by about noon if the traffic isn't bad."

iii

Pierre Duval walked into the Fleming Hotel and asked at the desk for the key to room 11. When he arrived upstairs, he unlocked the door, turned the knob, and pulled the door open, stepping into the room. With a long sigh, he walked to the dresser, laid the key near the lamp, and dropped his briefcase beside the chair. He laid his jacket and coat on the bed before dropping into the reclining chair. Phew! It had been a long, stressful day since he had gotten up early to catch the eight o'clock train at Waterloo Station that morning.

Isaac had driven him to this hotel in Dunklesland from the train station in Dorchester, obtained a room for him, and then driven on to a secluded but palatial villa and introduced him to his friend, Achmed. The man had a vaguely Middle Eastern–sounding last name and spoke slowly with a strong foreign accent. He had talked generally about the state of affairs in the world and more specifically about the war in Afghanistan.

Putting off any detailed discussion, he had invited them to lunch with him and a few associates, who joined them as they assembled around the large table in the next room. They were introduced; all had almost unprounceable names and were also dressed in casual western-style clothes.

Two white-coated waiters moved silently as they brought course after course. The meal was sumptuous, but Pierre found that he couldn't really enjoy it as the questions came steadily about his background, his interests, his current research project, and his views of Middle Eastern economic and political situations— especially on his views about the events of 9/11 and the war in Afghanistan.

It wasn't strange, in a way, that they were interested in his former French nationality, since in recent years the French government had been more liberally minded toward political developments in the Middle East than the other European countries, and definitely more so than the United States had been. And it had given him a feeling of satisfaction they had taken so much interest in his role as a teenager with the French underground at the end of the war. The idea of fighting against overwhelming odds to overcome the Nazis seemed to find favor with all of them.

Thinking about Isaac, Pierre reached into his breast pocket for his pack of cigarettes, shook one out, and lighted it. He glanced at his watch. *Where is Isaac? He said he'd drop by about now when he left the meeting shortly after lunch.* Pierre's thoughts were interrupted by a knock on the door. *There he is.* As he opened the door, Pierre could see that Isaac was worried.

"They really gave you a grilling, Pierre. I thought they were pretty well satisfied with the information I had provided, but they seemed to require confirmation of everything. How did it go after I left?"

"Let's go to the pub down the street for a pint and talk about it," replied Pierre as he picked up his key and reached for his jacket. "I thought it was a very interesting session, but I'm not sure that Achmed got much for his money."

They settled at a table toward the back of the room at the Red Lion and placed their orders. The pub was quite small but crowded with locals clustered around the bar. A dartboard on the wall beside the end of the bar was the center of a noisy game. It was smoky and a bit loud, but not too much for their conversation.

"After you left," Pierre began, "they showed lots of interest in the Nuclear and Plasma Sciences Society. I told them it is only one of the thirty-nine societies of the Institute of Electrical and Electronic Engineers. I explained that the Society sponsors conferences and its journals are commercially available in the U.S. Further, my own fields of interest in radiation detection and monitoring instrumentation were only a small part of the many fields of interest in the Society."

"That was included in your resume, as I recall."

Pierre nodded, "Then Achmed asked detailed questions about the International Atomic Energy Agency's inspections of Iraq's nuclear program both before and after the Gulf War. I told him it was my opinion that Iraq was planning to build nuclear weapons; but that's general knowledge, and it's been in the public press."

"Of course."

"Achmed seemed to lose interest in Iraq, but then he asked for more details about my recent visit to CERN. I told him the visit was related to my research for my current project and I wasn't in a position to discuss the study any further."

"I had made that very clear, as you recall."

"Yes, I do. Then over tea we chatted rather amiably about my work on atomic weapons development in the late sixties, a long time ago—ancient history. But it was pleasant recalling those days at Los Alamos. Achmed said that a car would pick me up at the hotel at ten tomorrow morning. He asked me to come back for a second meeting in the morning. A driver dropped me off at the hotel not long before you knocked at my door. What do you make of it all, Isaac?"

Lost in thought for a moment, Isaac signaled the bartender for a second round and replied, "Seems to me they're going through a lot of detail to assure themselves you have the qualifications they're looking for. Based on your work on risk assessment, it sounds like they're looking for help in nuclear weapons development."

Stopping to light a cigarette, he continued, "I wouldn't be surprised if they were looking for someone to work on-site somewhere in the Middle East. It must be pretty remote, even isolated, since I haven't heard of any active work being done during my time in Italy. I'm pretty sure they're willing to pay handsomely for the talent they want. They may offer some time to think about it, but I imagine they're considering making you an offer it would be difficult to refuse."

Pierre said, "It would have to be very substantial before I'd even consider dropping my research project, especially now that the president's War on Terror is so high on the national agenda."

"I'd guess the basic considerations for accepting such a position might be your willingness to live abroad, at an almost uncivilized location, for a government that might be on America's 'bad guy' list, at a very high salary and for an unknown period of time. You also have to think about the status of your current project and Nicole's ability to live under such conditions."

Pierre said, "And one thing I'd add to that list would be my own national pride, which would forbid me to work on anything that might possibly be a threat to the U.S."

Isaac added, "One puzzling thing about this situation is Achmed's presence here in Britain. During Desert Shield and Desert Storm more than ten years ago, British ground forces made a considerable contribution to the success of the campaign to eliminate Iraqi forces from Kuwait. I would have thought that foreign nationals of Middle Eastern countries would have been seriously questioned as possible security risks here in England. I really don't know how long he's been here or whether he's on any kind of security watch list. He may be an accredited representative of a foreign government, but I'm not sure of that."

"During our discussion this afternoon he seemed to hint at being associated with an embassy, but it wasn't clear to me."

"With your French background, American education and experience, I think they'll find you a very attractive candidate. There may be some more questions tomorrow, but I'd guess that Achmed will make you a firm offer. Since you don't seem particularly enthused at the idea, you might thank him for his consideration, ask for a week to think it over, and tell him that you'll call me within a week with your answer. Here's my card with my phone number, and here's your check for the two hundred pounds, as promised, no matter what decision you make."

Isaac continued, "I'm staying here at the hotel in room 19. I'll be out all day tomorrow, but I'll drop by your room again in the evening at six o'clock to see how it went—and will drive you to the train station in Dorchester the following morning, if you leave that day."

"That sounds just about perfect, Isaac," Pierre said, reaching for his glass to finish the last swallow of stout.

"Let's head back to the hotel for dinner."

iv

Barbara Brent, sitting at a table in the Beauregard dining room, pushed the dessert plate back an inch, reached for her coffee cup, finished the last swallow, and motioned to Miss Brown for a refill.

"Just a half cup will be fine," she said with a smile. Waiting for the waitress with the coffeepot, Barbara glanced around the room. Almost all tables were occupied, but it was still early, she noted. As Miss Brown poured, Barbara said casually, "I haven't seen Mr. Smith recently. Has he been coming to the dining room?"

Looking thoughtful for a few moments, the waitress replied, "Yes, he's been coming to breakfast very early, just as we open the doors, and as I recall, he seems to be coming in very late in the evening, having to rush his meals before we close up."

"I see," said Barbara with a smile. Still thinking of Charley, she reached into her purse, found her cigarette case and unconsciously opened it. She took a cigarette out, lighted it, and watched the smoke before she suddenly remembered the sign that proclaimed in large letters, "No Smoking," and quickly snuffed it out in her saucer. Looking embarrassed, she pushed back the chair and walked toward the dining room entrance.

Susanna Brice, sitting at the front desk beside the registration area, looked up and smiled as she approached. "I almost forgot you had a no smoking dining room," Barbara said with a mild grimace. "Just remembered in the nick of time."

"Yes, well there are the lounge and the front terrace," said Susanna with a smile.

Reaching for a pen on the desk, she asked, "Are you more comfortable since we moved those suitcases out of your room and into the storage area?"

"Yes, indeed. Thank you for getting them out of the way," Barbara replied. "I'm still pressed for closet space since I have too many warm weather clothes right now, but I'll manage."

"Speaking of clothes," Susanna said as she stood up, "I've been admiring many of yours. They look very comfortable and are quite colorful. The designs in the fabrics seem clearly Arabic. Did you buy them in Morocco?"

"Yes. I was very fortunate over the years to have been in a number of the Peace Corps's programs—so I worked not only in Rabat but in Fez, Marrakech, and Meknes."

"Did you have trouble finding your sizes?"

"Not really. Many of them are hand-tailored. There are very few stores like we have here, but the major hotels have a good selection."

"Have you ever been to Casablanca?"

"I wasn't there too often, but it's an interesting town; and as I recall, I bought a few things there. What I bought depended on where I was working. I was able to buy clothes in the north, in the mountains near the Algerian border where it was cooler, as well as closer to the Sahara at Marrakech."

"You have a great selection of colors."

"Yes, the fabric designs and colors are quite different since the people are a mix of Berber, Arab, and Black cultures."

"How did you manage with the languages?"

"Of course I didn't speak Arabic or any of the Berber dialects, but our interpreters and translators were always very helpful. I did study Arabic and French, and I learned enough to get by without problems."

"If you have a few minutes, let's go into the lounge. I'd like to hear more about your life in North Africa," said Susanna. Getting a nod from Barbara, she said, "I'll ask Miss Brown to bring us some coffee. Go find us some chairs, and I'll be right with you." She moved to the desk and placed the "Ring Bell for Service" sign up on the counter.

A bit later, moving slowly through the revolving door, Charley Smith nodded to Dr. Franklin, another resident, and started toward the dining room but then noticed Barbara and Susanna in the lounge and walked over to them.

"Good evening, ladies," he said with a smile. "Was on my way to dinner but couldn't resist stopping to say hello. Haven't seen you for a while."

He looked admiringly at Barbara, lounging back in her chair, cigarette in her right hand. She looked charming in her long, bright, burnt orange dress. Her earrings matched the color perfectly, and they went so well with the necklace of dark orange stones. Her curly dark hair was piled neatly on the top of her head.

Susanna was strikingly attractive in another way. Her graying, shoulder-length hair was pushed back as she raised her head. Even at the end of the working day, her crisp white blouse, choker pearls, and dark skirt looked very businesslike as she sat forward in her chair, coffee cup in hand.

"How's the acting business these days?" asked Barbara.

Smiling broadly, Charley looked at her and replied, "It's been a busy week. Quite a few companies have been shooting ad campaigns for the fall season. I've been doing voice-overs on a number of new products."

"Does it bother you that the audience doesn't see you? Just hears your voice?" Susanna asked.

Turning toward her, Charley replied, "Not really. My face has been seen in many ads, and face recognition is important; but advertisers have different needs for different products—for faces, voices, various age groups, and body shapes. So I'm happy to get involved in ads any way at all."

Addressing Barbara, he said, "I've been meaning to tell you I'm glad to see the U.S. and Britain working and fighting together in Afghanistan. We're wartime allies again, this time in a fight against terrorism. Those events on 9/11 were as uncalled-for as the attack on Pearl Harbor. Worse, another attack could happen at any time."

"I think all Americans are grateful for Britain's help," she replied grimly, looking at both Susanna and Charley.

He had perched lightly on the arm of a chair, but just then he rose, saying, "Well, I'm late for dinner. Better get moving, or they'll be closing the door," With a wave, he headed out of the lounge.

Raising one eyebrow, Barbara looked over at Susanna. They exchanged glances and a faint smile.

Placing her cup and saucer down on the table Susanna started to speak, seemed to think better of it, looked carefully over at Barbara, and started again.

"I want to hear about your experiences in Morocco, but first I have to ask, is this the first time that you've stayed in a residential hotel?"

"Yes. Why do you ask?"

"Well, perhaps it's just human nature, but it seems rumors are prevalent where guests are together over any period of time. Our entire staff is dedicated to eliminating unfounded whispers that seem to pass among the guests as soon as inaccuracies—sometimes even falsehoods—are identified."

"What kinds of whispers?"

"Sometimes the stories are true but are of a personal nature. Private. They're not necessarily the kinds of things that should be spread around—almost maliciously."

"Really!"

"Sometimes it's necessary for the management to be strict with individuals who, shall we say, *gossip* in a very nasty way. It occasionally leads to hard words and hurt feelings."

"I see. I can understand the problem."

"The reason I mention it is because I've seen you frequently with Colonel Johnson."

"Yes."

"Shortly after he arrived here, it was whispered around that he had been asked to leave the service due to gambling debts. I talked with him personally. He denied the story."

"Oh."

"The problem persists, so occasionally you may hear intentionally loud conversations, meant to be overheard, casting aspersions on his character. I've had discussions with a few of our resident ladies who are convinced the story's true and cite their knowledge as coming from unidentified sources inside the British Army."

"That's terrible."

"Has he ever mentioned it to you?"

"No."

"Well, I just wanted you to be aware that gossip and gossipers exist here as elsewhere in this sometimes unkind world of people," said Susanna as she picked up her coffee cup and saucer. "We'll get together on Morocco later." She turned and walked toward her desk.

Barbara sat lost in thought. She was becoming quite fond of Glenn Johnson. He hadn't mentioned why he had left the service. No reason to. He certainly never mentioned gambling. He'd turned down her suggestion to go to a London casino. *Hopefully, the story isn't true*, she thought. She'd have to raise the subject tactfully somehow.

Her thoughts shifted. And now this letter from Morocco. She thought she had ended her affair with Abdul very smoothly; their last night at her apartment in Rabat had gone well. She had been exhausted after their bouts of sweaty lovemaking, and she'd been sure he'd understood it would be their last time together. She remembered they'd had some steamy times, but she had been determined to get out of Morocco and leave that torrid affair behind. She hated the way Muslims treated women. She'd been able to avoid getting entangled with his beliefs and wanted to get back into the western world.

But he's so young, she thought. *Why is he following me?* She had seen him with younger women. And his wife was attractive. Before they'd met, she'd felt it would be difficult for an older widow to attract a young, vigorous sex partner. Now, he'd somehow traced her from her last address in Cleveland. *Damn! How to keep him from coming here?* She took the envelope from her purse, took out the letter, and quickly read through it again. Her only choice would be to check out and leave if he did show up—one thing she didn't want to do now that she and Glenn seemed to be moving toward a closer relationship. One damned problem after another.

Her throat felt dry. She wanted more coffee and looked around, but there was no server in sight. She got up and walked over to the windows, her mind in turmoil. She turned, walked back to her chair, and sat down again. Her thoughts turned again to Glenn Johnson. The first few times they were together, they had talked about his army career. She'd thought at the time that he seemed a bit vague about his finances, but why he was living here in London in a residential hotel?

Lost in thought, she picked up her cigarette case and lighter and got up again. She lit a cigarette, dropped the lighter on top of the case, and walked slowly toward the windows again. Her mind drifted back to an earlier dinner with Glenn. She had thought his explanation about being separated from his wife wasn't very clear, although she had gotten the idea the wife had chosen to live in Newcastle until some sort of unsettled estate matter was resolved. And then later at the door to her room, as they said good night, his light kiss on her cheek seemed almost brotherly, friendly enough. And his hand smoothly, lightly, touching her left breast as he reached over to kiss her had seemed accidental. But as she thought back about it, she felt their relationship was becoming closer, moving toward one she would like, and one too important to have Abdul appear here at Beauregard House.

She returned to the table, sat down, and crushed out the cigarette in the ashtray. She had an idea. She'd talk to Susanna and tell her that she was afraid Abdul would cause trouble if he arrived here. If another letter arrived, Susanna could stamp it "Addressee Departed. No Forwarding Address. Return to Sender." A post office solution!

She picked up her cigarette case and lighter, dropped them into her purse, stood up, and headed toward the front desk.

Chapter 5

i

John was seated on a chair on the Beauregard terrace. He had finished jogging around the Serpentine in Hyde Park, showered, and eaten breakfast and was resting comfortably, glancing through the Saturday morning paper as Madeline walked out through the revolving door.

Tapping him on the shoulder, she said with a smile as he rose to greet her, "It's too bad that there's no easy way to hire a car except by riding out to Heathrow airport to pick it up, but at least we have a nice sunny day for the trip. Are you ready to go?" She shifted a small package to her other hand, in which she held also her purse.

He dropped the paper on the chair and looked at her with a smile of approval. Her streaked blond hair was pulled back with a bright yellow bow holding it in a small ponytail. She looked relaxed and happy in a light yellow blouse and black slacks, a lightweight black sweater thrown loosely over her shoulders.

"Let's go," he replied, slightly raising his left elbow in invitation. She slipped her arm through his as they walked down the broad stairs and started toward Bayswater Road to catch the bus.

ii

The car had been rented in her name, so Madeline was driving. They were satisfied with the compact gray Ford. They had followed the signs out of the airport and were moving ahead nicely on the M25; traffic was not too heavy.

On the way to the airport, they had chatted about their activities during the past week: John's visits to various parts of the city with the sales manager, late dinners, evenings at the office with buyers coming in after business hours, which parts of the new line were selling in with the highest sales figures, comments about the customers he was working with, and opinions about the sales locations he had visited.

Madeline's side of the conversation was also Marallon-oriented: her continuing work in the photo studio, work with Louisa Hastings on the storyboards, discussions about her promotion schedules after product deliveries to stores began, and the UK national advertising campaign starting to run on television.

Regarding her personal appearances, Tim Campbell and the sales management team at the Marallon marketing department had tentatively booked her into major department stores in the Greater London Urban Area, then into West Midlands, Greater Manchester, West Yorkshire, and Greater Glasgow, the five areas with the highest populations; but specifics would depend on each store's promotion plans.

They had been driving for quite a while before their conversation turned to their coming visit. John said, "Why don't you tell me a bit more about your grandmother? You mentioned she's the one who counseled you about getting out of modeling and considering a career in business. Does she have a business background?"

"No," Madeline replied with a little laugh. "She was born and raised in Glasgow. Her father was in the beer-brewing business, but she grew up with somewhat of a distaste for beer. I think it was because of the somewhat rowdy business associates her father frequently had as guests at home."

Glancing over at him, she continued, "Actually it was a very loving home; she had devoted parents and a carefree childhood. Nevertheless, her private schooling took her away from her home environment, and by the time she reached the sixth form, she had come to realize that she wanted her life to lead in other directions."

After pausing to overtake a car, she continued, "She graduated with a degree from the College of Arts and Social Sciences at the University of Aberdeen. Degree in hand, she went back to Glasgow and started working in the field of social services."

She hesitated for a moment. "I really don't know what she did in her early years, but it wasn't too long before she met a graduate student of theology from the University of Glasgow."

Leaning forward over the wheel, Madeline pulled her sweater off her shoulders with John's assistance.

"From what my mother told me about her early childhood, Gram married my grandfather when he was ordained and successful in obtaining an associate pastor position in an Anglican church in Glasgow."

She continued, "So, my mother was raised in a fairly strict family environment; but she was the youngest of three children, and it was a loving family."

Smiling over at him, she said, "I guess I could digress here and tell you about Mother's life; but continuing about Gram, my brother and I were taken to visit Gram and Granddad at their home in Glasgow almost every year when I was growing up."

"As we got older, Mother would take us shopping on Sauchiehall Street. It was a real treat for us kids. Granddad was pastor of his own church when I was in my early teens."

After stopping to recall the date, she continued, "Then in 1982, Argentina invaded the Falkland Islands, and the war started. Granddad felt very strongly about the military casualties and led a volunteer group into the war zone. He had quite a hassle with the army in getting permission to go. His departure for South Georgia Island was the last time we saw him. He was fatally wounded in an air raid attack. Of course, his body was flown back and interred in Glasgow."

She seemed lost in thought for a few moments, and then looked over and smiled rather grimly.

"Gram took his death very hard. The children were grown and gone by then, so she felt terribly alone. Over the years, she and Granddad had developed friendships with a number of church families from Cambridge; so about the end of the first year after his death, she sold the house and relocated there. She had friends; she was closer to our family; and the weather was considerably milder." She paused in thought for a few moments.

"But we're getting close to the turnoff for Trumpington, so could you check the map, please?"

As he pulled the map out of the glove compartment, she went on talking. "Gram lives near Queen's Road, so it's only a short walk to cross King's Bridge to the chapel at King's College, where she attends every Sunday."

It didn't take long from Trumpington. In a short while, Madeline pulled the car into a parking place not far from her grandmother's house.

iii

Gram opened the front door on the third ring of the doorbell. Smiling broadly, she stood there, arms open wide to Madeline. As they embraced, John could see she had snow-white hair and a pink, crinkled face.

Over Madeline's shoulder, he looked at her bright blue eyes; and in the noonday sun, he saw she was dressed all in black with a white, lacy shawl wrapped lightly around her shoulders. She was delighted to see them both, and as Madeline introduced John, Gram took his outstretched hand in both of hers and said in her warm and friendly Scottish burr, "It's a pleasure to meet you, John. Please come in."

She turned and led them into a front room filled with period furniture that seemed to perfectly match the subdued turn-of-the-century exterior of the house.

Madeline dropped her sweater onto a chair and walked slowly around the room.

"It's nice to be back, Gram. It seems like a long time since I was here last, but everything's warm and cozy, just as it was." She handed the small package she held to Gram as they all sat down. Gram unwrapped the gift as Madeline continued.

"Mother and Dad—and Brother Jack, too, of course—send their love and affection. Dad and the local Conservative Party are still quibbling about the latest Labor education policies, but Tony Blair seems as popular as ever in Brighton."

"Thank you, Madeline," said Gram with a nod of her head. "Very thoughtful of you." She let the gift wrapping fall to the floor.

Sitting back in her chair, Madeline said with a smile, "I thought your ladies group from the chapel would appreciate some chocolates from Harrods's specialty shop."

She added, in reply to a question from Gram, "Yes, Mother is still in good health except for a little arthritis in her hand. But she's becoming more and more active with her volunteer and social programs."

"But you both must be hungry," Gram said, rising and starting toward the kitchen. Madeline followed.

"What can I do to help?"

Left by himself, John got up and wandered slowly around the room looking at the collection of family photos on the large desk, on the mantle, and sprinkled in front of the books in some of the bookshelves.

He stopped in front of the Anglican cross on the wall and examined the photos arranged around it of Gram's late husband in various church and family settings. A few large paintings of mountain scenery, displayed at appropriate locations on the walls were reminiscent of Scotland's Grampian peaks and confirmed the family's northern origin.

The call of "Come and get it!" brought him to the kitchen. The roomy breakfast nook kept the light lunch cozy and informal, conducive to John talking casually about himself, his boyhood in Stourbridge, his athletic days at college, and a bit about some of the consulting projects he had worked on previously.

Madeline added to the conversation with reminiscent scenes from her life following the inquest over the accidental death of the fashion photographer she had been working with in Brighton, some funny events at fashion shows, and her reasoning behind wanting to start a new business career.

Gram's questions and comments in her heavily accented Scottish burr kept the conversation lively, intimate, and friendly to the last scone and second cup of tea.

The women laughingly pushed John out of the kitchen as they bustled around cleaning up the lunch dishes. He went back to the study, which was just off the living room, and quickly became interested in the remembrance items, souvenirs of travels abroad, framed photographs, and portraits of Scottish family members he found there.

In the closeness of their kitchen work, Gram and her taller granddaughter talked more intimately of family affairs in Brighton, of relatives on Granddad's side of the family, and of Madeline's hopes for the future.

Madeline was particularly sensitive to Gram's inquiry about her long-term relationship with Wendell, and was cautious and somewhat evasive about her feelings for John, as Gram spoke of him. They discussed his coming assignment in Tokyo and what could result from the possible three-month separation.

By the time the last dish was placed back in the cupboard, they were talking about Gram's health. Even though she seemed hale and hearty, her age was starting to account for medical problems, and it was getting difficult to manage living alone.

John had never visited Cambridge, so Gram's offer to lead them on a short walk down Queen's Road, across King's Bridge, and onto the grounds of King's College was a welcome opportunity to do a little sightseeing.

Saturday morning classes had dismissed, so with the exception of a dozen or so couples punting on the river, there wasn't much student activity on campus.

Gram had lived there for so long she was able to give them a brief thumbnail sketch of the university's history, a bit about a few of the thirty-six colleges, some short stories about a few of the famous graduates, and impressions about the preparations underway for the celebration of its eight hundredth birthday, to be held in 2009.

On the way back, Gram led them into the King's College Chapel. The architecture was magnificent, and in the dimness of the sanctuary, as Gram went to the front pew and knelt in silent devotion, John and Madeline sat together across the aisle from her, each aware of the close bond beginning to bind them together—but at the same time, fully aware of their responsibilities to other potential partners.

The feeling of closeness, of quietness, persisted as they left the chapel and retraced their steps to Gram's house through the late afternoon sunshine.

It was time for cream tea and scones, making tentative plans for a Christmas visit, messages of love and affection for the Brighton family, and finally, emotional good-byes.

As the visitors stepped into the gray Ford and closed the car doors, Gram, speaking quietly, bid them Godspeed with a fervent wish for their safe journey, peace, and happiness for the days and years ahead.

iv

On the way back to Trumpington, there wasn't much conversation in the car. Each seemed to be rethinking the visit and making sure they were on the right streets to get back on the M25 again. After turning onto the motorway, they settled back in their seats, relaxed, and started to talk about the visit, about Gram and her Scottish burr, about the Cambridge campus, and finally about Marallon's new product launch again.

Madeline said, "You know, John, I really liked working with Louisa Hastings and the products in the new line. I was thinking of telling her that I thought the cosmetics industry was missing a big untapped market—teenage fragrance."

Looking over at him, she continued, "The whole perfume industry seems focused on women between twenty-five and thirty-five, the 'dating' group, and those women who have good jobs with money to spend on themselves, who are most likely to want a particular fragrance to tell their story during intimate situations."

"I think you're right."

"Maybe it's because I've been working with young models over the years, but I think teenage girls want to impress their peers, not necessarily teenage boys."

"That's interesting."

"And they aren't keen on heavy scents like musk and jasmine, but I think they'd go for lighter, more natural fragrances like spring flowers, or even a dash of melon, ruby red grapefruit, or a spritz of vanilla—new scents that are wholesome, pleasant, natural, and really aren't sexually oriented."

"And most teens can't afford—and wouldn't want—high-priced perfumes in a designer crystal; but they could afford a fancy eau de toilette in an eye-catching bottle, and they could even collect them like boys do baseball cards."

"Sounds reasonable."

"I guess the bottom line is, after my personal appearance program is finished, I'd really like to join the product management group in Mr. Campbell's marketing department as a junior product manager."

"They have two juniors now, so another one would be very possible."

"I don't have any experience, but I know the market, the potential customers, and I know I could work with the agency to come up with copy ideas. Also, perhaps a fragrance R&D

company to develop a sample survey … possibly a test market to check out the concept and packaging design."

Her eyes were glowing with excitement as she turned her head to look at him.

"What do you think, John? Is the idea too fantastic?

Do you think it would be out of line to talk to the marketing director instead of Helen Connors, the personnel manager?"

"I'm not sure, but I don't think so."

"Should I wait until the first personal appearances are complete, so I can talk from a position of success—provided they're successful, of course? And I really don't want to talk to any of the current product managers or the agency. Somebody may steal my big idea. Of course, the idea may have been tried before and failed to be successful. What do you think?"

"Wow," he said with a broad grin. "I'm really impressed. You really have been thinking about a new business career. I'm proud of you, and I think it's a great idea. You may be right—teenage fragrances may have been unsuccessful in the past, but you'll never know unless you do a bit of research to find out."

"What kind of research?"

"I think if you can make a case that it hasn't been tried before, it would strengthen the idea. If it was unsuccessful, then knowing when and why it failed would help you and the company to decide whether to pursue it further or not."

"Where could I look to find out if the idea has been tried before? Do you think that magazine research might turn up some answers?" she asked.

"Seems to me you could spend some of your spare time in the next few months at the library looking through magazine files. Build your case before you say a word to anyone. You could write it up like you did class projects at Exeter and boil it down with times, dates, and places to make it air-tight and convincing."

"I've been looking at women's magazines since I was ten years old, and I don't remember ever seeing anything like teen fragrances—not like what I have in mind."

"It would be most impressive if you had data from world markets, too. There may be interesting facts to explore in French and Scandinavian magazines, as well."

"I see what you mean," she agreed.

"When you have a well-documented case you're satisfied with, I think a direct approach to Tim Campbell would be the right way to go. Don't be discouraged if you don't get a positive response from Tim. He'll have his hands full for months with the new product line."

"I can see that already."

"More important, I'm not sure whether Marallon considers cosmetics, skin care, or fragrances to be its strongest product group."

"I'm not sure either … yet," she said with a broad smile.

"So you should look at other cosmetics houses at the same time that you're researching teenage fragrances."

"I see."

"The way forward may not be easy. Some companies want to be the first to market new ideas or new products, but some are reluctant. They want to be the first 'second' to market a product. The marketing philosophy here is to let someone else take the risk to test the market; then, if it's a success, be the first to jump in and try to grab a piece of the new market."

"Marallon always seems to be coming out with new lipstick colors, but I've never noticed whether they're first with new seasonal colors or not," she said thoughtfully.

He went on, "I don't know Marallon well enough to know which marketing philosophy it has. So, in the final analysis, it seems to me that you should do just enough research to get a feel for whether teenage products have been marketed or not. Don't spend too much time before going to Tim with the idea."

She nodded slowly, glanced over at him briefly, and then said, "I see. Sometimes things aren't as easy as they appear. I'm glad I mentioned it, and thank you for your opinion. It gives me a better handle on the idea, but do you think there's really some chance that Tim would hire me as a junior product manager without any experience?"

"Well, it's hard to say. As you said, you know the market; you have a good education; you'll have a good grasp of the proposed product line; and he already knows that you're industrious and hard-working, so I think you have a pretty good chance," he said with a big smile.

"And I have to say you're also a very good driver. Here's the first sign for the turnoff to Heathrow. It looks like we'll make it back to the Beauregard before they close the dining room."

"Good," she said. "I'll be hungry by then."

He continued, "And I'll have plenty of time to review what I've been able to pull together from what I learned at Ramsgate, to finish my weekly report—and get set for my staff interviews next week. It's been a great day, meeting Gram and spending the whole day with you, Madeline."

She looked over, reached for his hand, and said quietly, "It's been fun, John. Maybe we can spend some time sightseeing here in London during the next few weekends."

V

At Beauregard House, Glenn Johnson and Barbara Brent walked out of the dining room and into the lounge.

"That was a tasty meal," Barbara said as she and Glenn settled into two chairs beside a low coffee table.

"Yes, it was," he agreed. "Now, would you like an after-dinner drink, or coffee perhaps, like you had last evening?"

"Sherry would be nice for a change. Thank you, Glenn," she said as he got up and headed for the bar.

She watched him as he walked away and liked what she saw. She thought to herself, *He looks very nice this evening. His gray jacket goes well with his black slacks and almost matches the color of his hair. And he has such a trim build ... broad shoulders and narrow hips ... He's an attractive man.* She glanced around the lounge. There was quite a crowd by then, since they'd had a late dinner. She lit a cigarette and was exhaling the smoke languorously as Glenn walked up. Placing her drink on the table in front of her, he sat down in the chair next to hers and sipped his brandy.

"Have you made any decisions about the kinds of volunteer work that you'd like to do since we talked about it last week?" he asked.

She answered, "Not yet, but I've made a number of inquiries. And I've been to the library a number of times. I'm really not that interested in working with children again for a while. I've just about decided to hold off on the volunteer work until I can decide whether to make a serious attempt at writing a memoir of my work in the Peace Corps. During my years in Morocco, I kept a casual diary, a collection of thoughts on what was happening or what seemed important. It's been six years since Frank passed away; and during those years, I stayed very busy in Morocco, not only to keep the gloom away, but to avoid thinking about the future without him."

Pausing, she turned a bit in her chair to face him more directly. "But you know about that. We've talked many times about my work there, and quite a bit about your military assignments, but you haven't told me much about yourself or your family."

He looked over at her, smiled, and said, "No, I guess I haven't." Then, moving closer to the side of his chair, closer to her, he started talking quietly. "Well, you know I was born in Manchester." She nodded.

"I guess it was a pretty ordinary childhood. My brother Brian is two years older than I am, so I was always the little guy in the family. We lived in a big, old Victorian-style house. You know the kind: built about the turn of the century, red brick and wood, bay windows and balconies, a sweeping porch around half the first floor, chimney pots, the whole bit. We lived with my grandfather there for a number of years. It was near Heaton Park, a nice part of town."

"Sounds lovely."

"I don't remember much about primary school except that Brian and I walked to school—at least when the weather was good. Beyond that, we went on to a private secondary school that had an excellent sports program."

Sipping from her sherry glass, she asked, "Were you good at sports?"

"I always liked track and field very much, but then I got interested in football and played a lot. So, by the time I reached the University of Manchester, I was pretty good. In fact, in my last year at university, I was considered for a spot with the Manchester United football club. I hate to admit it, but I really took it hard when I wasn't selected. My girlfriend at the time was somewhat relieved I wasn't going to turn into a professional athlete."

"Why so?"

"To her, professional sports were too insecure, always a chance for a permanent injury, no real job security."

"I agree, in a way, although the successful ones make lots of money. What kind of job did your father have?" she asked.

"He ran the family business. It was inherited from his father's side of the family. Over the years, it grew into a cotton textile manufacturing company. The textile business was a growing part of Manchester's economy after the First World War and even more so after World War II."

"And your mother?"

"Mother was always involved in women's activities at the church, at local charities. She was outstanding at needlework—knitting and crocheting, especially—and was active in a businessmen's wives' group, spending more and more time helping the growing number of poor families as Manchester's textile business began to decline."

"Did you consider getting married after you left university?"

He hesitated, thought for a few moments, and then said, "No. We weren't all that close, and when I started as a traveling salesman for our company, my weeklong sales trips seemed to cause both of us to lose interest."

He talked about his early years following university, more about his work in sales traveling throughout England for the family business as he and his brother took over more responsibility as his dad aged, and then, about his decision to join the army while his older brother assumed overall responsibility for the family business.

"When did you get married?" she asked quietly.

He didn't answer. He sat back in his chair and ran both hands through his hair. He took a cigarette from her case on the table, lighted it, and let the smoke out slowly as he turned and looked at her.

"I married the daughter of my commanding officer when I was stationed in Germany in 1990. It was before Desert Storm, and we hadn't been married very long before the regiment's deployment to Saudi Arabia. Actually, I hadn't known her very long before we married. She had been raised in a military family, of course, and had lived many different places as her father was transferred. She had known army officers her whole adult life, and I'm not sure we knew each other well enough before we married."

"So, your wife remained in Germany when you went to Arabia with the regiment?"

"Yes, but so did all of the other military wives."

He went on to talk about combat operations in Kuwait, the defeat of the Iraqi Army, and the regiment's redeployment back to Germany in March 1991. His mouth and throat were getting dry. He went to the bar to refresh their drinks, and then sat down and began to speak haltingly and vaguely about his wife's involvement with a fellow officer.

"What do you mean 'involvement,' Glenn? Do you mean she was having an affair?"

"I'm really not sure how long they knew each other, nor the extent of the involvement, but it chilled our relationship. It was whispered to me that they were seen at a number of different places. Apparently, it began while I was with the regiment in Kuwait and went on even after we redeployed back to Germany."

"But how could you stand it—not knowing what was going on?"

"Well, it never reached the point of breaking up our marriage. Nancy never admitted any wrongdoing, and I never wanted to force an admission that would tear us apart. I did become aware that we were drifting apart as I began to spend lots of my evenings at casinos trying desperately to win enough to help Brian keep the family business afloat during hard times."

"When did you begin to gamble?" she asked.

"Well, I was very good at mathematics in college. Dad liked to play poker very regularly with business associates. They were always friendly games, and I enjoyed watching them in my late teens. Then later, a group from the college football team began to play regularly. So, when Brian and the family business needed financial help, it seemed natural for me to try for larger stakes. I could play at the casinos after my duty hours, and I was moderately successful in winning enough to be helpful in the business."

He lighted another cigarette, took a deep puff, and let the smoke out slowly as he glanced around the lounge. Then he went on.

"The market for textiles in Manchester continued to shrink until the cotton market closed in 1968 for lack of business, followed by the closing of the Port of Manchester in 1982 when supertankers and container ships had grown too large to use the River Mersey and the Manchester Ship Canal." The colonel's face took on a pained expression as he described his decision to leave the army when criticism from his friends over his gambling became too much to bear.

"Nancy was absolutely brokenhearted about my leaving the army recently, but by then my potential army pension supplemented my gambling success, making me essentially independent of my annual salary. I could afford to go off active duty. I had told her that I was really struggling to end my gambling since the family business had improved and didn't need my assistance. But by then, we couldn't agree on a place to live."

"Why not?" Barbara asked.

"Well, I've always favored urban living right here in London, but she has her heart set on looking for a place near Camberley. It's right near the Royal Military Academy Sandhurst. Her father had been stationed there more than once while she was growing up as a young girl. She has fond memories of the place, and we seem to have reached an impasse over how and where we can ever get back together again. Anyway, at the moment she's staying in Newcastle with her mother, who's engaged in sorting out an estate problem on her grandmother's side of the family."

He finally stopped talking, glanced at his watch, and looked around the now deserted lounge. "Well," he said, looking at her directly, "it's getting late. It's not a happy story. I can't believe I've been talking for hours."

She looked at him and couldn't say a word. It seemed like such a tragedy, starting from such a fine beginning. To hear the misfortune continue—the early end to his military career, the apparent end to his marriage, his struggle to end his gambling—was shattering to her ideas of life and love. Her eyes were moist; she was almost in tears. She got up from her chair, reached for her purse, opened it, and dropped her cigarette case into it.

"I just don't know what to say, Glenn." She reached for his hand as they walked toward the lift. The lobby was deserted, the lift door standing open. As they rode up to her floor, not a word was said. She reached into her purse for her door key. The lift door opened, and they walked hand in hand along the hall to her room. She unlocked the door, pushed it halfway open, and looked up. Their eyes met—and held. She pushed the door open, and they both walked in. She closed it behind her and turned the lock.

Chapter 6

i

Pierre Duval walked restlessly around his room at the Fleming Hotel. He glanced at his watch again. Where was Isaac? He reached for a cigarette and lighted it as he walked to the window. It was a very pleasant view, lots of trees, a wide back lawn, but it did nothing to relax him. He had been at the hotel since early afternoon, had gone to the pub, reread the morning paper, and done some writing. Now he was impatiently waiting to head back to London. There came a knock on the door. Ah! There he is. Right on time.

Pierre walked quickly to the door, opened it, and cried out heartily, "Glad to see you, Isaac. Come in."

As they sat down in the chairs by the window, Isaac asked, "Well, how did it go today?"

"Just about as we discussed last evening," was Pierre's reply. "Achmed was alone. There were more questions, mainly focused around my present research project, for example, what kind of demand did it make on my time, when would it be finished, how long would it be before I would be ready to take on a new exciting challenge, what was my reaction to our residing abroad under difficult living conditions, and so forth."

"What was your reaction?"

"Negative. But then he got down to specific work examples that I might encounter if I were to accept the position that he had in mind. By this time I had pretty well decided that I wasn't interested, but he finally made an offer that I had to think twice about."

"Why? Was it the money?"

"It was a very tempting offer: very good salary, assurances that I wouldn't lose money on the sale of my house in Washington, moving expenses paid for, a long-term contract with paid vacations to get away from the work area each year."

"Was the location specified?"

"No, but as he talked, it seemed to me that the living conditions would be difficult for Nicole. And in the final analysis, I really didn't like the idea of working for a Middle Eastern government, even if it was camouflaged under a corporate name—especially now with the war going on in Afghanistan. I'd feel like a traitor."

"Well, I really don't think he's representing one particular country. I think he's acting as a free agent, receiving a commission for each successful candidate he finds. A small independent headhunter company working in highly technical fields," said Isaac.

Pierre nodded. "I finally said I couldn't make a decision right away. I had to discuss it with my wife, needed more time to make a more specific estimate about when I could complete my current project, before I could give him an answer. Achmed began to get very angry. He controlled his temper, but I could see that he was very unhappy with me."

"Did you feel threatened?" Isaac asked.

"I really did begin to wonder whether I'd get out of there in one piece. We walked outside to the car, and the driver brought me back here."

"What have you been doing since then?"

"I had lunch at the pub and did some writing. And I've been pondering whether I did the right thing. Now I'm really in a quandary. The money would be very good, but I know Nicole is not very flexible about living conditions. What really concerns me is the use made of my research efforts. I could never take the job if I felt I was contributing toward a weapons development program controlled by a government that supports terrorist organizations. But I might never know if I were working for a foreign company whose real identity was obscure."

"What to do? A little time may not be enough to help me make a decision. What do you think, Isaac? Is there any way that I can get more information about the company or the government Achmed is working for? In our discussions, we only dealt with technical areas of research. He did say there would be adequate translation and interpreter assistance, but he carefully avoided talking about where the research was to be carried out. The discussions about location were so vague that the site could have been Iran, Pakistan, or even North Korea."

"I doubt we'll be able to get any more information," Isaac replied. "My contacts provided just enough facts for me to locate you on your way back from your meeting in France and enough direction to guide you here. I'm afraid you'll have to make a decision about whether you'll take the money—probably more than you could make anywhere else—and take the risk of being labeled a traitor, possibly ending up in a CIA book of 'bad guys,' or just drop the whole idea and return to your project."

Impatiently snuffing out his cigarette in the ashtray, Pierre said, "Well, that's about the way I see it too. I have some time to think about it before I decide. Anyway, now you're here, I'd like to get started back to London."

"Well," Isaac said with a tight smile, "I kind of had a hunch you'd want to start back this evening no matter what you decided about the job. I stopped at the front desk on the way up here to check the train schedule. If you check out now, I can drop you off at the station in Dorchester in time to make the next through train to London. You can have dinner on the train and be back at the Beauregard before midnight."

"Sounds perfect," Pierre said. "I'm already packed." He stood and reached for his suitcase, briefcase, hat, and jacket. "Let's go."

ii

At Beauregard House, the night manager was at the front desk as Pierre pushed through the revolving door into the lobby. Nicole was still reading in bed as he unlocked the door, walked into their room, and dropped his briefcase and suitcase beside the chair.

In a tired voice, he said, "Surprise, Nikki. I made it home one day sooner than expected."

Laying her book aside, she quickly got out of bed and hurried over. They hugged warmly. She kissed him, looked anxiously up into his eyes, and then asked, "How did it go?"

He kissed her, and then shrugging out of his jacket he replied, "About as we discussed—more money than I expected with no real assurance that we'd be going anywhere except somewhere in the Middle East." Pulling down the knot of his necktie and unbuttoning his cuffs, he sat down in the chair as she sat on the bed.

"I told them I couldn't decide whether to take the job until you and I talked and I had a chance to review my project. The real problem, what really worries me, is not knowing whether I'd be doing research for an enemy government, since the name of the employer wasn't really made clear…"

"Well, enough about the job. Isaac Wentz met me. You remember Isaac from DOE. He was very helpful. I have a feeling I don't want to decide until we're back in Washington. I expect I'll call Isaac when we get home and tell him I'm not interested in the job, but I'm still not sure."

"Anything new here while I was away?" he asked as he started to take off his shoes.

"Not really," said Nicole. Nothing important. I had a long talk with Barbara Brent about her experience in Morocco, and also with Madeline Claiborne, that model who's working for Marallon cosmetics. Very interesting women."

With that, she got back into bed as Pierre got up and walked into the bathroom.

iii

In his room at Beauregard House, John reached over and turned off the alarm. "How could it be 6:00 AM already?" he groaned.

Turning on the water in the shower, he was glad he'd taken enough time last evening to finish his weekly report. *Yesterday was so pleasant*, he thought. *The trip to Cambridge, the visit with Gram, dinner and the evening walk with Madeline.* But he knew it was time to get back to work.

After hanging up the towel, he glanced at his watch as he put it back on. It was not too late to slip into his running outfit and spend the next half hour doing a slow jog down to the park and back, not so fast that he'd need another shower.

After returning from his run, he changed his clothes and was still early for breakfast. He missed seeing Madeline on his way out of Beauregard House but made it right on time for his first staff interview with members of Marallon's London headquarters.

In many ways, it seemed somewhat of a repeat of his interviews in Ramsgate but with much less of a global view of the company's business and a more focused overview of the UK and Europe.

During the next few days, again using his management audit principles as he had done at Ramsgate, John was able to quickly work through the financial aspects of the business—

the accounting, budgeting, cash and credit management procedures—with ample assistance from senior staff.

The rest of the week flew by as he worked his way through other functions, including production management, inventory control, and billing procedures in the plant at Brentford. Then at Marallon House, his focus shifted to marketing strategy and sales management control, with very early breakfasts and extra-long hours of interviewing during the days, and long evenings of information consolidation back in his room at the Beauregard.

And the next week was just as busy. It started on Saturday with calls on local key accounts with the sales manager, Mike Ryan. Then, on Sunday, they started north to give John an overview of accounts in different circumstances.

The trip was actually a regular quarterly inspection trip by the sales manager to assure himself that regional sales reps were adequately handling their local customers. Monday morning they called on major accounts in Glasgow and Edinburgh before continuing on to Aviemore and a number of smaller accounts along the way to Inverness. On the way back to London they made sales calls on accounts in Wrexham and Cardiff in Wales before stopping at department stores in Bristol and Exeter in the West Country. It was a very strenuous but very productive two weeks.

On Saturday morning, John was pleasantly surprised to see Madeline come into the dining room as he sat over his late-morning coffee after a brisk jog through the park. With a smile, he motioned to her to take a seat as he lifted the morning newspaper off the table in front of him.

"Hi there. How have things been going?" he asked.

"Just fine," she answered warmly. She smiled as she pulled out the chair and sat down. "The commercials are finished and edited, and I've been working with the agency on the specifics of my personal appearances with the major department stores. It's been a very busy time."

"And it's been hectic for me too," he sighed. "I'm about ready to relax, to walk around a bit, to see some of London. Care to do some sightseeing?" he asked.

"I'm glad you asked," she replied. "And the weather's perfect to see some of the interesting sights around town. This is really the first time I've ever been here long enough to see any of the famous places. I bought a tourist book just this past week, and I think I'd like to start with Westminster Abbey. How does that sound to you?"

"Great. I've already had breakfast, so you go ahead and eat while I run up, shower, and change my clothes. I'll be back before you finish your coffee," he said.

She had finished her meal and stood up by the time he came back to the table.

"Ready," she said with a smile as she picked up her sweater and small purse. "I've always wanted to see the Poets' Corner."

Taking his arm, she continued, "I've read Chaucer and Dickens in school, and Gram read us poems by Robert Burns as children. I want to see their memorials, and of course, Walter Scott's and Shakespeare's." They went down the stairs from Beauregard House and started for the tube stop at Lancaster Gate.

It was a short walk from the underground stop at Westminster to the Abbey, and they chatted about walking across Westminster Bridge to get in line to ride the London Eye after finishing all there was to see in the Abbey. And then, while the long view of the city from the top of the huge Ferris wheel was great, nothing could beat the view of the Thames they saw while strolling back across the bridge and along Victoria Embankment. The underground from Charing Cross took them to St. Paul's Cathedral, and from there they traveled three short tube stops to Tower Hill for a walk among the Tower of London Beefeaters and to take a look at the royal jewels.

It proved to be an interesting and vigorous full day's journey. They ended it with an underground ride from Tower Hill to Piccadilly Square for a bite to eat and then an evening's rest on the public benches under the leafy trees in Leister Square where they enjoyed the mildness of the setting sun.

Reaching for his hand, she said, "It's been a fun day, John. Thank you for going to all the places that I wanted to see today. If you're game for another day, tomorrow we'll go see what you choose. How about it?"

"You're on," he said, "but you may be sorry you let me choose the places because I'm basically a museum crawler. We'll go first to Buckingham Palace to see the Changing of the Guard, then stroll down the Mall to Trafalgar Square and go into the National Gallery. There are feature presentations, plus all of the standard masters. You'll love it."

"Sounds great," she said.

"Then we'll have to ride the tube to South Kensington station. I'd like to browse through the Science Museum, and the Victoria and Albert Museum, which is close by. And then, if you're still able to walk, it's not far to Kensington Palace where Queen Victoria lived during her early years. How does that sound?"

"Wow! Overwhelming, but fair's fair; and I'll get to see some of the things that interest you, so it's worth the effort," she replied.

"Now let's go back to the trattoria at Lancaster Gate for some ice cream before it gets too late."

They had done a lot of walking and so agreed to turn in early and to meet for a late breakfast, since the Changing of the Guard at Buckingham Palace was not scheduled until eleven thirty. It was a good move because they both felt a bit tired the next day as they finished their morning coffee and started for the tube and the ride to Green Park.

It was a lovely Sunday morning as they walked down past Lancaster House and along the Mall. They arrived in front of the Queen Victoria Monument just as the New Guard arrived from Wellington Barracks.

Arm in arm, they watched as the Old Guard handed over the sentry positions, and afterward they strolled with the crowd moving down the Mall as the New Guard marched to St. James Palace, leaving the detachment at Buckingham Palace. Then, hand in hand, they continued along the shady Mall to Trafalgar Square and on into the National Gallery with its colonnaded entrance and attractive dome.

At the gallery's snack shop, they stopped for a coffee break.

"That was a long walk from the palace," he said, "and the time is flying. This is one of Europe's finest art collections, so why don't we find the Impressionists collection and find a few of the most famous paintings by other artists. Then we can come back here for a sandwich before heading for the Science Museum. Or maybe we can just walk around the corner and visit the National Portrait Gallery. I'm afraid I selected far too many things to try to see in one day."

"I'm not really tired," she replied. "Let's carry on with our original plan—at least until I get foot-weary," she said with a smile.

They found the Impressionists, a dozen or so paintings of other famous artists, and then had their lunch break. They crossed Trafalgar Square, stopping by one of the fountains to gaze up at Nelson's statue on the top of his column, after which they headed for the Charing Cross tube stop and the ride to South Kensington station.

There wasn't much of a crowd at the Science Museum, so they moved among the major exhibits fairly quickly. But by the time they left the museum and crossed Exhibition Road to enter the Victoria and Albert Museum, they had run out of time, and it was too late to go in.

Walking back toward South Kensington station, they found a small restaurant and had a leisurely dinner before returning to Lancaster Gate.

They walked along Gloucester Terrace toward Beauregard House and again stopped at the trattoria. As they sat down at one of the small tables, the Italian waiter with the cheery voice came up, and they placed their order. In the quiet semi-darkness of early evening, the lighted candle on their table threw a soft glow on Madeline's face.

"It's been a wonderful weekend, Madeline. I can't tell you how much it's meant to me. I hate to think about leaving for Japan, feeling about you as I do. But we both have commitments to others right now. My trip will give me a chance to free myself from mine."

"I know what you mean. And I'll be thinking along those same lines," she replied.

"I'm scheduled to return to England about mid-August. I expect that I'll be finished with the Marallon assignment by that time, or later, so I may not be in London then. But I'll meet you in Trafalgar Square on the gallery side of the Nelson Column at twelve noon on Sunday the first of September or under the entrance to the National Gallery if it's raining."

She nodded.

"If you're there, I'll know that you're free too. Does that sound like something you'd like to do?"

She sat there quietly, looking at him. She reached across the table for his right hand, looked him straight in the eyes, and spoke gently.

"Oh, yes, John. I've known since our visit to Gram that you were going to be more than a casual friend. And the time that you're away will give us both time to think about our significant others and about the future. We seem to have so much in common I feel certain that we'll be happy together."

He was elated and could barely refrain from leaning across the table to kiss her, but his dish of ice cream and the lighted candle stopped him. He barely noticed what he was eating as they both finished. They sat talking for a while until he finally realized that he had an early flight in the morning.

"I'm scheduled for two weeks in Ireland, but I think I may need less time there," he said. "I expect to head for Tokyo as soon as I return from Dublin, but I'll make sure to see you before I leave. If you're finished, let's head back to the Beauregard." With a nod, she pushed back her chair and joined him as he handed some money to the waiter on the way out of the trattoria.

It was quiet along Gloucester Terrace as they walked slowly hand in hand back toward the hotel. The occasional overhead streetlight dimly lit the sidewalk. It was darker under the tree as John stopped, gently swung her around in front, threw his other arm around her waist, and hugged her. He gently kissed her warmly on the lips.

She didn't resist and shyly returned the kiss as she threw her arms around his neck. Feeling his hardness against her body, she stepped back.

"No, John. You're not just an affair for me, and we both have other obligations at the moment. I'll miss you terribly while you're away, and I'm already thinking of our meeting again at Trafalgar Square on September first—when we're both free."

"Until we meet again, then," he said as they continued on their way. At Beauregard House, they pushed through the revolving door and kissed goodnight as the lift door opened.

iv

In his room the next morning, John reached over and turned off the alarm. "How could it be 4:00 AM already?" he groaned. Turning on the water in the shower, he was glad he'd taken a few minutes last evening to finish packing. The weekend had been just about perfect—Westminster Abbey, the London Eye, St. Paul's, the National Gallery, and Madeline—but now it was time to get back to work.

After he had finished his shower, it was still too early to eat at the Beauregard, so he decided he would grab something at Gatwick before boarding the flight. He dressed quickly and, with suitcase and stuffed briefcase in hand, stopped at the front desk to drop off his key, and then headed for Victoria Station and the Gatwick Express. He used the thirty-five minutes on the train to review his Dublin schedule and boarded his flight after a "breakfast bacon egger" at one of the airport "fast fooders."

He had gotten a window seat as requested, and as he settled back in his seat, he finished off the last of his coffee. As he looked out at the clouds, part of the previous evening's conversation with Madeline floated back into his mind. He wasn't sure how it had come up in their conversation. They were talking about her experiences in the modeling profession when it just seemed to pop out as they were sitting over lunch at Gram's.

She'd said, "They haven't all been pleasant. In fact, one or two were downright frightening. Some time ago, I was working on an advertisement for a clothing manufacturer who was introducing a short line of 1890s dresses as a special promotion, a college fad at the time. I had worked with Aaron Wisket, the photographer, on many occasions, but this time he liked the idea of a living room setting with antique furniture, including old-fashioned oil lamps with tall glass chimneys."

She paused, thought a few moments, and then continued. "I was seated in a chair beside a small table that had a lighted lamp standing on it. Behind it was another lamp, a floor lamp adding light to the scene. I was to stand and turn with a flourish to show an organdy dress with a white lace collar and a flaring skirt."

She stopped, then, breathing deeply, went on. "Aaron was on a ladder focusing his camera, looking down slightly on the scene, and as I rose, he turned slightly to follow my movement, slipped off the ladder, and fell right onto the table, breaking the lamp and spilling oil all over his arm with fire spreading up into his hair. I was absolutely stunned, and the flaming oil spread quickly as his assistant and I tried to pull him out of the flames."

She stopped, put both hands over her eyes, and rubbed her forehead slowly with both hands. "He was badly hurt, unable to help himself as we struggled to drag him from the wreckage. It was awful! There wasn't anything in the study to smother the flames. I finally pulled the seat cushion off the chair and struggled to beat the flames from his head. It seemed to take forever before we had the fire out, but it was too late. Aaron was fatally burned. The hospital emergency room could do nothing to save him."

She stopped and sat back in her chair, putting her hands to her forehead again. After a few moments, she continued. "There was an inquest looking into his death. Franklin Wilson, the young assistant, and I were questioned and praised for our efforts to save Aaron, and it mercifully ended my publicity nightmares over the accident. It was months before I could get the picture of Aaron in flames out of my mind."

She finished her story with a shudder, as if she were almost reliving the horror.

John's mouth was dry. The roar of the engine out on the wing brought him back to his seat in the cabin. He glanced at his watch and said yes to the stewardess who asked whether he'd like another cup of coffee.

The landing at Dublin airport was smooth, and he felt their time in the air had passed very quickly. As he pulled his suitcase off the revolving baggage carousel, he thought to himself, *Now, where's Brian Donovan? He's supposed to be here holding a sign with my name on it. Ah, there he is. Perfect timing.* He made his way toward the tall Irishman with the shock of black hair, ruddy face, and hearty smile.

"Thanks for meeting me, Brian; I appreciate your taking the time."

"Glad to meet you, John. I'm looking forward to showing you our little operation here. I hope you'll find it useful. Been here before?" he asked as they moved toward the parking area. He was dressed casually and spoke with a bit of a lilting Irish brogue, not at all heavy.

"No, I haven't. My first time."

As Brian cleared airport traffic and headed toward Dublin, he said, "I've booked you into a small, classic hotel on O'Connell Street not far from the corner of Parnell Street. You'll be right downtown—plenty of places to have dinner in the evenings. I personally prefer this small hotel. It's got the feel of a family home, much better than the large commercial places. I hope you feel the same, John. But I can easily cancel and put you elsewhere if you prefer."

"Sounds fine," was John's reply.

"You'll get to know the folks who run it. They're a very friendly couple. Name's O'Sullivan. There's plenty to see in the center of the city and across the River Liffey to Trinity College. I hope you get to know our city during the week you're here."

"I'm looking forward to it."

"You'll be well oriented as you take off for your next week in Belfast. Being close in, you won't need a car. Everything's within walking distance. I'll have someone pick you up each morning and drop you off in the evening."

"I appreciate it," John said with a nod.

"Actually, you're not going to have much free time. We have a small research group that works with two start-up biochemical companies. They're looking for new ingredients. Hopefully, they will help us to develop new products. Might change the entire concept of skin care."

"Sounds interesting."

"We have a number of production lines primarily to fill bottles and jars that we buy locally to cut product cost—less expensive than shipping finished products from our London factory."

"Makes sense."

"We also compound a few products from ingredients shipped over from London. Preserves the privacy of the ingredient mix. And of course, we have a marketing manager and his team, plus the accounting, finance, and reports section."

"I see," said John, nodding.

"You'll spend part of one day with the sales manager, calling on a few key accounts and a few small independents. And, you'll have time to talk with our staff. Your interviews in Belfast will be mostly import- and distribution-oriented and will allow you time to summarize what you've learned so that you can ask any unanswered questions before you return to London."

"Sounds good, Brian."

"This afternoon after work, I'd like to take you home to meet the wife and have dinner with us and the children."

"Thank you. I appreciate it," John said with a smile.

"Tomorrow morning, Patrick O'Shea, my production manager, will pick you up at the hotel about 7:30 and bring you out to our production facility at Clontarf. It's located near the port and not far from the international airport, a very convenient location. Pat lives on the south side of the city and can pick you up on his way to work without going out of his way."

"That's great. Thank you."

"Open the glove compartment, John. Take out the folder—it's yours. It has our organization charts, floor plans of the building, a company telephone directory, a product listing, a product price list, and a copy of the most recent Marallon audit report about our operations here in Ireland. There's enough in there to get you started today and to bring you right up to date on production, inventory, and billing procedures by the time Pat picks you up tomorrow morning."

Nodding, John took the folder. He was still glancing through it as they pulled up in front of the Southern Hotel. Stuffing the folder into his briefcase and taking his suitcase in hand, he followed Brian into the lobby. It was just as Brian had described it, rather small, clearly family-run, with a homey appearance.

Mr. O'Sullivan himself sat at the front desk and confirmed the booking. He reached for a key as John signed the register.

"I'll be down in a minute, and we can be on our way," John said as he started toward the stairway to his room on the second floor.

V

With Brian at the wheel, John briefly described to him the background of his present assignment—the three murders of Marallon dealers in Tokyo, the thorough investigation by the Tokyo police, and their inability to solve the crimes or even to find convincing motives for any of them. Traffic was heavy, so there was relatively little conversation as John explained the Tokyo managing director's feeling that it was too much of a coincidence that no one from Marallon had been found to be involved. He was not convinced, and his request for an independent comparison between the UK company's operations and those of the Tokyo subsidiary, had resulted in his current assignment.

"Interesting. Thank you, John. I understood you were studying our operations and I was to fully cooperate in your efforts, but I didn't realize the second half of your study would really be more important than the first half. You're really not here to help us but rather to examine our methods as thoroughly as possible in the short time you have. Sounds like a tough job. We'll try to explain our work as completely as possible. Well, here we are," he said as he pulled smoothly into a parking space in front of the Marallon Dublin building.

They walked into the building, said good morning to the receptionist who was already at work at her desk, and went up to Brian's office.

A number of the staff had already begun to assemble for the regular Monday morning meeting, so there were handshakes and greetings as the team began to pull up chairs around the front of Brian's desk.

Looking around at each face in the group, he said, "I've scheduled John to spend a bit of time with each of you during the week. He's working for the head office in London and will be leaving for Belfast on Saturday, and then off to assignment in Japan, so he won't have much time."

He's here to get a detailed overview of our operations, so please answer all his questions. He'll be using a desk in the accounting office and has a folder full of details about our organization.

Pausing, he looked around the table, and then continued. "Unless there are any questions, let's proceed as usual: production, sales, accounting, and any personnel problems," Brian said as he opened his production folder.

The meeting ran for over an hour as events facing the company were aired, discussed, and resolved, so it was close to 9:30 by the time John was escorted to his desk in the accounting department, where he shook hands with the folks sitting nearby, found the location of the nearest coffee and tea station, and began to assemble his case study of Marallon's Dublin operation.

The folder Brian had given him was a great start; he arranged the data in the same way that he would in preparing a management audit of a small manufacturer. In the fifteen sections of his draft audit running from accounting to taxes and legal obligations, there were lots of gaps that needed to be filled, lots of questions to be answered.

He was able to get the leads he needed to move ahead from Twain Callahan, who had been appointed as his main point of contact for such inquiries. She had been working her way up in the accounting department for the last eleven years and knew everyone in the company due to her harp playing and Irish dancing, which she performed whenever a company party needed entertainment.

She was a popular person, and her impish grin, shock of reddish hair, masses of freckles, and ready smile made her pleasant to work with. Her knowledge of operations was such that John's questions were barely out of his mouth before she had the answers.

John was able to quickly pull together the basic accounting, budgeting, and cash and credit management procedures. He wasn't concerned with accuracy of numbers or auditing the details, only with an overview of the activities as a reference to what he'd find in Tokyo.

With Twain's help, he was able to find key personnel and conduct interviews to assure himself that operations were conducted as described in procedural documents.

After a brief lunch break, John felt that the afternoon flew past, and he was surprised when Brian showed up at his desk at 6:00 PM.

"Time to close the doors and head home for dinner. Ready to go?"

It didn't take long for John to shuffle his papers into a reasonable order and join Brian in his car on the drive home to dinner with the Donovans.

vi

Promptly at 7:30 the next morning, Patrick O'Shea pulled up in front of the Southern Hotel. John, standing outside near the front door, recognized the car from Brian's description, folded his newspaper, and headed for it.

Pat was a big guy with a rugged look, a mop of curly reddish-brown hair, and the lilting brogue of the Dublin-born Irishman. His blue work shirt was open at the collar, and he held out a ham-like hand in greeting. He pulled the car away from the hotel, and John noted that he seemed to be about thirty-five.

The conversations, introductory at first, turned to Pat's experience at Marallon, and then to John's dinner with the Donovans the previous evening.

"I had a pleasant visit with Brian and Mary last evening. They have a lovely home and children. Mary prepared some special Irish dishes that I'd not heard of before."

Pat smiled. "Yes, they're a nice family. And speaking of Irish dishes, I'd like you to join Anna and me for dinner at our place this evening."

"I'd like that. Thanks for inviting me."

Pat nodded, looked over at John, and said, "I've been told that you're here on a training assignment. Do you also plan to look for ways to improve our production operations?"

"No, there won't be time for that. I'm here to learn how you do things. It's a different kind of consulting assignment. Ordinarily, I'd be looking for ways to make improvements, and I'd develop recommendations."

With a chuckle, Pat said, "Often, recommended improvements are very tough to achieve."

Smiling in agreement, John continued, "As consultants we make recommendations based on our experience in similar business situations. It's management's job to improve production methods as resources become available."

"I agree. Frequently, we feel there are improvements that can be made, but it's not always easy to select the best approach."

"Of course, and it's not always happy times when we recommend organizational changes that damage careers and personal relationships."

"Much of the time, management knows changes are necessary but won't make them. They use a consultant's recommendations to justify actions they are reluctant to take on their own. It's a way for a manager to relieve his conscience, especially when people have been closely associated over time."

"I understand," said Pat. "During my years in business, I've been in two situations where management should have made changes, especially where women were concerned. They were reluctant to make the hard decisions needed to clean up the problem, and the business suffered—at least in the short run."

Their conversation turned back to the production schedule facing Pat and his department if they were to meet expected shipping dates as the new product launch plan proceeded. The sell-in sales results had been good, and initial launch shipments were being packed, ready to be released so product would arrive and get unpacked just prior to when first advertisements would be breaking.

The discussion of the launch date events took John's mind back to Madeline's schedule. As he looked out the window, his thoughts turned to her personal appearances to begin at Selfridges on Oxford Street, followed by a week at Harrods in Knightsbridge. He wouldn't have an opportunity to see her in action at the largest promotions in London but thought he might be able to catch her performance somewhere else in London before his departure for Tokyo. Now that she was focused on product management as a possible career opportunity, it was somewhat less important that she get top personality billing during the promotions.

Pat O'Shea swung the car neatly into a space in the parking lot at Marallon's Dublin plant.

"Traffic wasn't too tough this morning," he said with a wry smile. "I generally leave here about six, and I'll be happy to drop you off at the hotel each evening."

After a quick coffee break, they went for a walk-through of the production areas. As expected, product components, bottles, caps, and labels were already in position for the day's run, and while production lines were shorter than those John had seen in the London factory, the layout seemed a bit more pleasing. There was more fresh air, and the melodic sound of Irish tunes over the loudspeaker system added an extra spark of pleasantry to the filling line environment.

The attitude of the women who operated the equipment seemed more relaxed; and they appeared friendlier among themselves than the workers he had seen in London—but perhaps that was his imagination.

As they walked into the shipping department, Pat pointed out, "We're prepacking assortments of products for shipments headed for key customer accounts for the launch rather than trying to fill specific orders."

"Is that standard procedure?" John asked.

"The reason is that the product line is so new that the consultants behind the counters have no experience in knowing which shades of products and which sizes will be most popular. After the first few weeks of sales, after the ads break, and after some experience with personal appearance campaigns, the sales reps will work with each major account to adjust their stock levels, to replenish the fast sellers and relocate those particular products that are not as popular as our market research is indicating they will be."

Handing a sample order form to John, he continued, "We're rapidly piling up orders, ready to be shipped, in a storage area that we were able to set aside; but it's filling up in a hurry, so it's going to be a close fit."

Leading the way down one of the filling lines, Pat said, "We may have to start shipping a few days before schedule. Most customers don't have extra storage space in their stores, and they don't like us to ship early; so it's always touch and go for a while with new product introductions."

Satisfied that he had a good overview of the production floor and related operations, John finished the afternoon working on his management audit with more assistance from Twain. He had dinner with Pat O'Shea and his family that evening, and afterward, was dropped off back at his hotel.

Early the next morning, Tom McCain, the Dublin sales manager, picked John up at the hotel and took him on an eye-opening visit to a major account on Henry Street, followed by a stop at a key account across the River Liffey on Grafton Street.

Tom said, "You can't leave Dublin without seeing one of the most beautifully decorated manuscripts in the world, John." With the sure steps of a former Trinity College student, he led the way across the Trinity campus to the Old Library.

"This is the Book of Kells, the centerpiece of an exhibition that attracts over five hundred thousand visitors to the college each year."

In the quiet room, Tom whispered, "Written around the year 800 AD, the book contains a decorated copy of the four gospels in a Latin text. It's written on vellum in a script accompanied by whole pages of decorations appearing throughout the text. The manuscript was given to Trinity College in the seventeenth century."

Following a quick lunch at the campus student cafeteria, they went to Tom's office and reviewed the company's marketing and sales plan for the balance of the year.

The rest of the week flew by for John. He met with members of the research team and the contract company's representatives doing the actual laboratory work, and quickly reviewed the research results of the previous year; but it was clear to him that the expected breakthroughs for the development of new concepts in skin care were not on the immediate horizon.

He met with Brian Donovan and reviewed personnel management policies, relationships with the local office of the London advertising agency, annual marketing and production planning objectives, and annual budgeting procedures.

They also discussed the tentative plans for John's review of the sales and distribution system operating from Belfast in Northern Ireland, but after considerable analysis, they decided there wasn't enough new information to be learned there. They agreed to cancel the week in Belfast and allow John to return to London a week early.

He had a chance to enjoy downtown Dublin's pub scene one early evening with Tom McCain, who had a typical sales manager's fine appreciation for discussions over politics while "hoisting a pint" at friendly establishments frequented by local politicians.

By the time late Friday afternoon rolled around, John had assembled copies of everything he had gathered during the week into his Dublin audit notebooks and folders, and had completed and sent off his weekly summary report to his home office.

On Saturday, Brian, Mary, and the children took him to see Blarney Castle so he could walk up the traditional steps to kiss the fabled Blarney Stone.

On Sunday morning, he drove across Ireland with Pat O'Shea and his family to Galway Bay, to view the Cliffs of Moher and the scenery in the Burren, and then ended with lunch in Limerick. An afternoon ride to view the magnificent beach scenes along the Dingle Peninsula with a return to Dublin through Tralee and Kilarney finished John's week in Eire.

vii

After an early Monday morning flight from Dublin airport, John walked into Beauregard House, registered at the front desk, and took the lift to his old room. On the phone, because of the late Friday decision to cancel his week in Belfast, John had been able to convince Tim Campbell, the marketing director at Marallon House, to rearrange his schedule for the day. He then sat down at the table in his room for a few hours of concentrated review of all the data he had gathered since beginning the Marallon assignment.

During lunch and a long afternoon session with Tim Campbell, he discussed the audit reports he had assembled during his week at the Ramsgate office; the weeks he had worked with the Bond Street and Brentford factory staff in production, marketing, and finance; his visits with sales reps in England, Scotland, and Wales; and his overview of operations in Dublin.

"Well, John," Tim smiled. "It looks like you've done an outstanding job of understanding and documenting Marallon's UK operations. It's clear that you're well positioned to take a comprehensive look at Marallon Tokyo's operation. As you recall, the New York office is directly responsible for Japan's operations, but the parent company, Marallon UK, has agreed to take an unbiased view of the Japanese subsidiary and to reach a conclusion that will satisfy the managing director's basic question: are operational changes required or not?"

Reaching for a folder, Tim continued, "As you requested, our travel office looked for a flight leaving today or tomorrow and reserved a seat for you aboard Japan Airways leaving for Tokyo from Heathrow at seven this evening. It's getting late, so I'll have them bring the ticket up to our managing director's office."

Getting up from his chair and moving toward the door, he said, "Now let's go up and see him. He wants to talk to you before you leave."

"So, you're ready to leave us, John," said Simon Greene as he rose from his desk and extended his hand. "Tim has been keeping me informed of your progress and your reports have confirmed that you've absorbed the data our managers and staff presented during your stay with us."

"I assume you're satisfied with your final review, Tim," he said turning to the marketing director.

"Yes, Simon, I think John has done a professional job in summarizing the major functional elements of Marallon UK," he said with a smile.

"Splendid. As you know, the Tokyo police have concluded there's no evidence to connect Marallon Tokyo with the murders. But, the board of directors here agrees with Japan's managing director, and we feel obligated to make one last attempt to prove the innocence of the company and our employees."

"We hope that you'll be able to close the case by giving us a clean bill of health; but, on the contrary, if evidence exists, we want it revealed—and documented, if possible."

"I understand," John nodded. "It seems to me that the most obvious contact between the company and the retailers is the sales staff, and as I understand it, nothing has come from analysis of these relationships in the past; but I want to take a closer look before searching deeper. In any case, you'll be receiving copies of my reports. I don't plan to stay in Tokyo one day longer than necessary, and my return departure date will be as soon as the managing director and I have reached a conclusion, as agreed by our contract."

Rising, Simon said, "I know you're leaving later today, so best of luck, and I hope you have a good flight." He extended his hand.

"You'll be hearing from me, sir," John replied as he shook hands, picked up his briefcase, and turned toward the door.

He shook hands with the receptionist and, with another good luck in the air, closed the front door behind him and headed for the Bond Street tube stop.

At Beauregard House, he was disappointed to learn from Susanna Brice that Madeline was working at a Marallon promotion in Brighton and would not be returning to the hotel until Friday evening. He stopped to shake hands and say so long to Charley Smith and Barbara Brent who were sitting together in the lounge. Then, before leaving his room, he quickly wrote a brief note.

Madeline:

I'm very sorry I missed seeing you before my departure for Tokyo. I'm leaving on a flight at 7 PM this evening. I'm not sure when I'll return but I look forward to seeing you in Trafalgar Square by the Nelson Column at 12 noon on the first of September.

John

Chatting with Susanna Brice at the front desk, he said, "This is the first time that I have ever checked into a hotel and checked out before having spent one night. The travel office at Marallon took me literally when I asked for a flight today or tomorrow. I didn't realize they were so efficient." He smiled.

He left the note with Susanna as he paid his bill, and then, with bulging briefcase in one hand, he picked up his heavy suitcase with the other and headed for the Lancaster Gate tube stop and Heathrow airport.

Chapter 7

i

His flight was on schedule, but John still had enough time to call Hannah in Birmingham. They didn't seem to have much to talk about since John had been away for four weeks and Hannah was getting used to his not being there. No, he wasn't sure when he'd return, he told her, and yes, he would write as soon as he had an address.

John was assigned a window seat as requested, so he settled in comfortably as the plane headed north for his over-the-pole journey. He was a little surprised when the sky became lighter as the plane headed north over Iceland. The sun was shining as the frozen Greenland landscape appeared. Momentarily, he had forgotten the flight was approaching the Land of the Midnight Sun during this mid-summer season.

The meals were good, but it was a very long tedious flight over the Artic Ocean and the Russian Kamchatka Peninsula. John was able to drift off to sleep for a while, but like the other passengers, paced the aisle to get his cramped muscles moving every now and then. He had skimmed through his briefcase, refreshed himself on selected phases of his UK experience at Marallon, finished the *Financial Times*, and continued with his copy of *The Modern History of Japan*.

Finally, the Japanese island of Hokkaido appeared far off the right wing, and it seemed to be just a short time before the pilot instructed them to put their seats back into the upright position and prepare to land at Haneda Airport. The customs procedures went quickly enough, but he felt tired as his eyes searched for his name among the many signs held by the welcoming crowd. *There it is,* he thought, as he raised his arm to wave, *and that must be Mr. Higa, the marketing director.*

"Hello, Mr. McKay. I'm Makota Higa. Nice to meet you. How was your flight?"

"Very good, but a very long one," he replied with a smile. "And please call me John."

"I will, and call me Makota. It used to be a family name, but now it's my first name," he said, smiling. "It's a long walk to baggage claim. This way," he gestured as he started to make his way through the crowd. "Can I take your briefcase? It looks very heavy."

"No, but thank you for asking," John said.

Makota was taller than the average Japanese man but sturdily built, and even though he had a ready smile, his strong jaw line signaled that he was a determined, no-nonsense manager.

The baggage had not started to arrive yet, so they had a chance to talk about personal matters: how long Makota had been with Marallon, how many children he had, how old they were, where his family lived, that he had perfected his English while attending the University of California.

For his part, John discussed the time he had spent living and working in Japan as a young army officer, his familiarity with the Hibiya Park area, and his many walks through Ginza. "I'm glad to be back in Tokyo," he said, "and I'm looking forward to working here again."

They retrieved John's suitcase and then stopped at the bank office for currency exchange. As they walked toward the taxi line, Makota said, "Our head office is in the Shibuya area, in one of the newer office buildings. Like everywhere in Tokyo, the traffic is very heavy and slow-moving. We could put you in one of the international hotels, but you would have difficulty traveling to and from the office. As an alternative, we recommend you stay in a typical, family-owned Japanese hotel within walking distance of the office. The owners speak some English, not fluently, but enough to meet your needs."

"In addition to convenience, it would give you a chance to become more familiar with the way we Japanese live. You'd sacrifice international lodgings for a Japanese cultural experience. What do you think?"

"Great!" John replied enthusiastically. "Since I expect to be working internationally, I might as well start now to begin to adjust to cultural changes. I'm glad you suggested it, Makota."

"Alright, then. We'll go directly to the hotel and get you checked in. You can have either a western-style bedroom or a Japanese-style tatami-mat room where you sleep on futons and have low furniture, but you're familiar with that from your previous experience. In either case, you can have meals in a western-style dining room."

"Hmmm, I think I'll try the Japanese-style bedroom. I can always change rooms if I can't handle it."

The traffic was indeed slow, and John was feeling drowsy as they reached the hotel and dropped off his luggage in his room.

Makota counseled, "I know you'd like to lie down for a nap, but it's easier to recover from jet lag if you can force yourself to stay active and go to bed at your regular hour."

"Why don't we walk down to the office? I'll show you around the place, you can meet a few people, and then we can walk on down through the neighborhood to the main Shibuya shopping area. We'll return here for dinner. That should help to keep you awake, and that way, you'll also know how to come in to the office tomorrow morning."

ii

After breakfast the next day, John sorted out all the heavy stuff from his briefcase, locked it in his suitcase, and headed for Marallon Tokyo. The walk had been interesting last evening, but he was glad that he had been able to get to bed early.

He hadn't slept particularly well. The tatami mats weren't exactly hard, but they weren't as soft as mattresses either.

He had been surprised to learn that the managing director, Kinya Arakawa, was an American–born, second-generation Japanese American, a Nisei, and had been raised to speak Japanese at home by his parents living in Southern California; so he was fluently bilingual.

The long, three-block walk to the office with Makota was pleasant except for the traffic noise and the traces of automobile exhaust in the air, evident even at this relatively early hour. As he was led to the fifth floor, John understood why the managing director's office was in the back of the building, away from the street in front.

Having been briefly introduced last evening, John and the director were on a first-name basis. The three men sat around the director's large desk and quickly reviewed the summaries of the last two New York team's conclusions.

They also reviewed the police reports on the murders of the Marallon retailers. John had briefly reviewed the reports at Ramsgate but had then focused on the UK operations. So, he was glad to get this onsite review by the principals involved. It had been only four months since the last report had been completed.

"That's about it, John," said Kinya as he rose at the end of the review.

"Makota is your primary point of contact for anything you need to get started, but I've assigned an experienced interpreter and translator, Mr. Simitra Doi, to work with you as required. He knows he's to respond to you as you need him. You may take the detailed reports with you, and here's a copy of our general procedures manual in English that you may use."

As John reached for the folders, Kinya continued, "There's an office just off the receptionist area that you may use, and you may conduct interviews with our staff there as needed. Just tell

Makota who you'd like to interview, and he'll have his secretary arrange it."

"Sounds good," said John.

Continuing, Kinya said, "Generally, you may find it more convenient to interview our staff in their offices. My door is always open if you need to see me. Makota will keep me posted on your progress. Good luck, John."

As they walked from the director's office, John said to Makota, "The first thing I'd like to do is to take a more thorough walk-through of the offices here, then go take a look at the warehousing and shipping location, which you said was located in another building. The quick walk-through that we made last night was fine, but I'd like to meet the manager in each major organizational element so that I can return on my own with the interpreter and he'll know who I am."

"We can start right now," said Makota.

"Can you introduce me as working on a special project for the director and ask your secretary to make me a name tag with my name in Japanese?"

"No problem," Makota replied. "Let's go to your office now, drop off your documents, get your name tag, and then I'll escort you around. When we're finished, we'll go back to your office, and I'll ask Mr. Doi to take you to the other building."

"Sounds perfect," John said as they started toward the elevators.

By the time they finished the tour and returned to his office, John had again become accustomed to Japan's bowing tradition instead of the handshake, and he soon found himself at each new introduction, with his hands at his sides, almost bowing himself.

As they stood at his office door, John said to Makota, "It's gotten too late to go to the other building today. Please tell Mr. Doi that I'd like to leave here about 10:00 AM tomorrow to avoid the morning rush hour."

"Will do," Makota agreed.

John settled in at his desk, quickly sorted through the stack of documents, and focused on the detailed report dealing with the investigation of sales activities in the first sales territory where the murder had been committed.

Lunch with Makota was a very brief meal break at a close-by local restaurant, but he still ran out of time before he finished and had to leave for his hotel or risk getting locked in as the office closed its doors for the night. It had been a full day, and he was not completely over his jet lag; so he was glad to go to bed early again.

The next morning's visit to the warehouse and shipping office with Mr. Doi didn't yield anything new. It was about as John expected, but now he knew where it was located when he got around to a more detailed review.

On returning to his office, he continued his review of the reports concerned with activities in the first sales territory. He found nothing unusual or suspicious but continued his review of other reports for the next few days before turning to a comparison between the UK procedures and those of Marallon Tokyo that had been furnished by Kinya.

With the office closed on Saturday afternoons and Sunday, he and Makota were able to attend shows at the Takarazuka and Kabukiza theaters, and together with Doi-san, they visited the major department stores along Ginza. They also visited the Imperial Palace Plaza to admire the views of the walls and gates surrounding the Imperial Palace.

One afternoon, Makota asked John if he had spent any time at a geisha party during his last tour in Japan.

"No, I was a very young officer at the time, and our pay scale was pretty low back in those days. Actually, I didn't know any of our Japanese employees well enough to spend social evenings with any of them, and I'd heard that geisha were very, very expensive."

"You're right," Makota nodded. "They were—and still are—high-priced, but to celebrate the progress of your work here, I'd like to invite you and a few of our senior managers to dinner tomorrow night at a traditional teahouse in Shimbashi and have two or three geisha in for entertainment after the meal. They'll be wearing traditional, full white makeup with red lipstick and red and black accents around the eyes and eyebrows. Their colorful kimonos will have extravagant obis tied in back."

"Sounds very interesting," John nodded.

Smiling broadly, Makota continued, "In the old days, prostitute geisha tied their obis in front so that their garments could be taken off easily and often, but today, geisha are generally not in the sex business. I'll ask for one to be a young apprentice geisha. They usually speak English, learned in high school these days. The others will be older, will probably play the shamisen, and sing traditional songs and dance as well as tell jokes and flirt with the men."

The next evening, dinner and entertainment at the Lotus Tearoom went as planned. Makota had arranged for the geisha through the local geisha union office and was pleased at their appearance, looks, and talents. The evening had been quite wet, and their geta, traditional wooden sandals, were left at the front door as usual. The entertainers moved gracefully through the evening in their white tabi.

The apprentice was a very pretty girl, and John was fascinated by her eyes, which were enhanced by the black eye makeup. She spoke English haltingly but amused John with funny stories of the life of a young geisha in Tokyo's Hanamachi Shimbashi area. She sang lilting Japanese songs as she played the small shamisen she carried. Her professional name was Atsui Hana, which meant "warm flower." In a way, John was glad that he had not met her sooner, or he definitely would have liked to see her again, even though he wasn't quite sure what she would look like without her white makeup.

Not long after that evening, John began to be more alert as he walked around the city. Twice he had narrowly escaped being hit by what appeared to be a careless motorcyclist in the heavy traffic, just after leaving the office in the evening; and once had been pulled away from in front of a huge truck by an alert pedestrian. He began to wonder whether these incidents were coincidence or whether he might be getting too close to the problem at Marallon.

Back in the office, the days rolled by quickly for John as he focused on various functions: budgeting, financial reporting, sales management, and the personnel records of sales reps. He had been in Tokyo for almost three weeks before he found a major difference between the methods used in the UK and Japan to control customer billing.

A procedural weakness allowed collusion between one or more shipping clerks and at least one of the billing clerks. The procedure permitted shipments containing extra products to go to dealers without the full number of products being invoiced. Related to that, sales reps calling on customers never checked inventory at the counter and product sales against orders showing quantities of product delivered to the customer, as they did in the UK.

A kickback scheme could allow the customer to pay off the two clerks with some of the proceeds from the sale of the extra products. A greedy retailer, unwilling to kick back enough of the profit from the under-invoiced shipments, could conceivably be murdered by a warehouse worker or a paid assassin.

Inventory shortages would not be obvious until annual audits, and shortages could be attributed to breakage in incoming shipments, accidents in the warehouse, or inaccuracies in customs documents.

Keeping his suspicions to himself, John, accompanied by Doi-san and Minoru Fukamiya, the Tokyo sales manager, called on Hirata-san, the widow of the store owner who had been murdered in his own office the previous February. She had been working in the store full-time since her husband's death.

Prior to arriving at Star Bright Cosmetics, John asked Fukamiya-san to work very casually with one of the consultants who normally sold the Marallon line and to turn the visit into a regular sales call on the basis that the regular salesman was ill. He was to review the sales book record, the products in the cases, and the reserve stock, keeping a sharp eye peeled for what might be considered excessive amounts of very high-priced items, particularly fragrance products, without commenting to the consultants who worked for the store and were not paid by Marallon.

Leaving Fukamiya-san with one of the consultants, John and Doi-san sat down with the widow in the back room.

Had she been able to recover from her husband's murder? Did she have any more information or ideas about who might have killed her husband? And had she thought of any reason why he had been murdered—anything beyond what she had told the police in February?

No, no new ideas, she said; and yes, she had been able to recover with the help of her eldest daughter, who had taken over the financial records portion of the family business.

There didn't seem to be any more information to be learned, so after some general discussion about business along the Ginza, and leaving Fukamiya to finish his work with the consultant who generally sold Marallon products, John and Doi returned to the Marallon office. John made an appointment to see the managing director first thing the next morning.

iii

Assembling his notes and ideas that evening, John was prepared for a thorough discussion of his findings with Kinya Arakawa. After a cup of green tea was served at the managing director's desk,

John began with a quick summary of the company functions he had reviewed, where he had found no problems.

Focusing then on the shipping and billing operation, John said, "I haven't found any direct evidence that Marallon was connected with the murder of Haruo Hirata, but the Marallon process of filling an order by a stock clerk selecting products from inventory, placing the products in a shipping container, then sealing it before the contents are independently checked against the order, could lead to someone fraudulently including more items than ordered so that a customer receives more items than he's billed for. The same thing can happen if the contents are checked by someone in collusion with the shipping clerk. Then there's room for a kickback scheme for the store owner to pay off one or more shipping room employees from some of the proceeds of the sale of the over-shipped products. There's enough slack in the system that the items missing during an inventory check could be covered up with fake breakage reports and alleged customs discrepancies."

Getting no comment from the managing director, John continued, "It's not possible to check the inventory movement at Star Bright Cosmetics at this late date, so in my view, there's no way to prove that the weakness in the order shipping procedure was the basis for the last murder, and I think the murders will continue to be officially unsolved. Mrs. Hirata, the wife of the murdered store owner looked and acted frightened during our discussion. I couldn't tell whether it was because she thought that she might experience a similar attack, because she's afraid of Marallon or some other manufacturer, or simply because she's not used to talking with a gaijin."

"That's possible," Kinya said quietly.

Continuing, John said, "The present workers on the shipping lines can't be accused of anything without proof, and firing without apparent cause is unfair. But there is the possibility that there might be pressure for collusion if you were to add administrative people to the shipping and billing system to eliminate possible future product losses."

Kinya nodded slowly and said, "I agree."

John looked at his notes, paused, and went on. "You may want to consider a rotational type of training program that periodically moves workers out of sensitive positions in the shipping and billing cycle to other receiving, warehouse, or transportation jobs. That will require considerable personnel work to structure new jobs requiring the skills of current employees. If there is a kickback system in operation, those employees who lose money as they're moved out of current jobs may quit, so the company will indirectly solve the underlying problem."

Sitting back in his chair, John shook his head and said, "In summary, it seems almost unbelievable that such a simple error, or collusion, in the shipping procedure could open the door to theft and murder in a kickback scheme, but I can't find anything else that gets up close to a retail store owner like this. Would you like me to brief any of the staff on my findings?"

The managing director sat there at his desk lost in thought for a few moments. He reached for the small box near his calendar, took a cigarette from it, and lighted it. Gently shaking his head, he replied, speaking slowly and thoughtfully, "No. There are no absolute facts to support the possibility of collusion. I don't want to alarm the staff or the employees. I prefer to work quietly with the staff to begin to make changes in personnel assignments that should eliminate any possibility of such actions in the future. Also, in the future, inventory discrepancies will be more thoroughly examined."

After pausing thoughtfully, he continued, "I suggest that you complete your report along the lines you presented unless you can suggest another line of inquiry. I've been following your progress as you completed your analysis, and I want to thank you for your thoroughness and professionalism."

Looking directly at John, he went on, "I'm glad you completed the study and the result did not positively implicate any of our employees. I feel satisfied with the result. If there was collusion, the changes I'll make will assure the possibility is eliminated in the future. If there was a kickback scheme, I'm afraid that the murderer escaped, and the crime will not be solved."

John sat there listening quietly, without speaking. Finally, he said, "Alright then. I plan to finish my report over the weekend. Your managers can devise a training plan to move people off the shipping line. There's no need to include details of such a plan in the report. Besides, having your managers involved in developing the procedure, and knowing the basic reason for the training and retraining, may help them to recognize other potential problems."

He went on, "Finally, since Star Bright Cosmetics sells many other manufacturer's products, there's still no evidence Mr. Hirata's murder was caused by anyone related to Marallon. The fact that Marallon scarves were used in the first two murders may have been sheer coincidence; nothing related to Marallon has been proven."

Looking directly at Kinya, "I must confess, however, for a while I wasn't sure whether I was getting too close to Marallon's involvement with the retailers deaths."

"What do you mean?"

"Well, I was very close to having accidents as I was leaving here in the evenings. Twice, there were very close calls with speeding motorcycles, and once a very heavy truck would have crushed me if an alert pedestrian hadn't pulled me out of the way at the last moment. But I can't be sure these weren't simply street incidents, perhaps all too common in Tokyo's heavy traffic. And since I've not been personally attacked, and I've never felt personally threatened, I must conclude I was just being careless in crossing the street."

"Well, that seems to wind things up then," said Kinya Arakawa. "I'll accept your written report if it reaches the same conclusions you presented. I'll consider the investigation completed and the case closed upon submission of your report. Thank you again for your efforts. The uncertainty of any Marallon involvement has been very unsettling over the past two years, and with the changes in the shipping and billing procedure, the personnel shifts, and the training program, I believe we'll finally have some closure."

Coming around the desk as he spoke, the managing director of Marallon Tokyo shook hands with John and said, "Come back and see me before you return to England."

His last weekend in Tokyo was a very long one for John even though most of the report had been completed. Finalizing the last chapter and the executive summary, plus tabbing all of the attachments and making sure the report was ready to be taken back to London for approval and signature by the managing director of Worldwide Consultants UK, had taken the entire weekend.

Early Monday, he stopped in Kinya Arakawa's office for a handshake and to explain that he would be taking the report back to London for approval before mailing it back to Tokyo.

iv

John's return flight over the pole seemed just as long and as tiresome as the flight to Tokyo. It was the beginning of the last week in August, so the long daylight hours had been reduced considerably since late July. The landing at Heathrow was right on schedule; but the city traffic was heavy, and the ride back to Lancaster Gate seemed interminable.

It was just about dinnertime when John registered again at the Beauregard House front desk. He was not surprised to learn from Susanna Brice that Madeline had been checked out for the week and was expected to return from a week of promotional appearances in Wales by the end of the month.

He was also not surprised to see Barbara Brent dining with Colonel Johnson. After dinner, he found them together in the lounge, sitting around a low table just as Miss Brown was pouring coffee.

"Won't you join us, John?" asked Barbara as John paused to say good evening to them.

"Yes, I will. Thank you, Mrs. Brent."

Miss Brown reached back to her tray for another cup and saucer for John. Choosing the chair closest to Barbara, he sat down with a question addressed to her.

"I've been wondering why you're still 'Mrs. Brent' but there's still no Mr. Brent in sight after all these weeks."

With a little laugh, she replied, "Yes, I can understand that. When we were living in Morocco, my husband was working for a German company there. He passed away about six years ago, and I haven't been able to forget him and haven't wanted to drop my married name."

"But Glenn here," she said, nodding toward the colonel, "is trying to help me remember I'm a widow, so please call me Barbara."

With a smile, Glenn Johnson, dressed in a light gray turtleneck sweater almost matching the color of his hair, said, "That's true." He reached for her right hand, which was resting on the arm of her chair.

"Barbara's far too young to be lost in the past. Life is to be lived in the here and now. It's time for a fresh start, for enjoying the sunshine in the park, and for dancing during these fine, late summer evenings."

"I agree," said John with a hearty smile.

"But where have you been?" she asked. "It seems like months since we've seen you."

Nodding his head, John answered, "Actually, it has been a long time. I was traveling in Scotland and Wales before spending a week in Ireland; and then it was more than three weeks in Tokyo, but the time there seemed to fly."

"Had you been there before?" she asked.

"Yes, a few years ago, and it was interesting to be back in Japan again. But it seemed strange that news of the war in Afghanistan seemed very low-key in Tokyo."

"What do you mean 'low-key?'" she asked.

"Well, pictures of American casualties made it to the front pages, but combat coverage was very light even in the English language newspaper. Among the Japanese where I was working, there was strong sympathy because of the damage the terrorists had caused in America, but not a lot of support for the war."

Turning to Glenn Johnson, he said, "The war news is pretty important to me. I'm still a commissioned officer in the reserve, and if things turn grim, I guess I could be called back to the army."

With a nod, the colonel replied, "I know the feeling."

John continued, "My time here at the Beauregard is coming to a close. I have a couple of meetings tomorrow, and then it's back to Birmingham the day after."

"Well, we'll miss you," Barbara said as she placed her empty coffee cup back on her saucer. "I hope we'll have a chance to say bye before you leave."

With that, she stood up and reached for Glenn's hand as he also rose. He put his arm around her, and they started slowly toward the TV set in the middle of the room.

John stood up, wandered out of the lounge and back to the revolving front door. He pushed through it and stepped out onto the front terrace. It was a pleasant late summer evening. There was still plenty of light as the sun was setting, so he walked down the steps and headed toward Hyde Park.

He walked slowly, thinking of Madeline. He was looking forward to seeing her. It seemed as though it had been a long time, but her face was vivid in his memory as he thought of their reunion. Was there any possibility that she wouldn't be at Trafalgar Square on September first?

There was always the possibility that she had changed her mind, that the attraction of her significant other in Brighton had been too strong, that she had forgotten him. He was tempted to call Marallon in the morning, find out where she was and call her, but on second thought, rejected the idea.

They had agreed that they would not be in touch until that magic day when they'd be reunited—provided they both showed up at the appointed hour. If they were both there, it would mean they were no longer committed to others. They would be free to be together without feeling sneaky and without cheating on previous commitments.

He was going back to Birmingham in a few days, and he was hoping his last meeting with Hannah would go smoothly. They had been going together for the past year, but they'd had some unpleasant times when she seemed to be too demanding of his time. Their relationship had become more difficult as his vision of expanded work in the management consulting profession had conflicted with her desire to have him nearer than he could manage on a number of occasions.

This had been the longest they'd been away from each other, and he could not help feeling that he had broken the chain that seemed to bind him to her. He thought they truly loved each other; but her possessiveness made him uncomfortable, and at times he'd wished he wasn't tied to her quite so tightly. Actually, he felt relieved about that. And though he was sorry to part from her in a way, he was convinced that marrying would be a mistake for both of them.

By this time, he had reached the Pied Piper statue in the park. He stopped, took a good look at it, and sat down on a bench close by, facing the lake. He thought back to his training program at Marallon UK. It had been extremely helpful in his analysis of Marallon Tokyo's operations; and he felt his conclusions were correct—and that the managing director's dissatisfaction with the situation had been settled.

He was confident that the personnel and procedural changes in the Tokyo billing and shipping areas would put to rest any underlying fears. In the future, employees should not be able to get involved in similar crimes. *But*, he thought, *where there's a will, there's a way.* Acceptance of managerial responsibility and vigilance, not reliance on a written procedure, were the keys to good performance.

A few ducks were moving slowly not far from the edge of the lake, seemingly looking for a quiet place to settle for the night, as he rose and started back toward the park entrance. His thoughts shifted to what new project might be facing him as he returned to the Worldwide Office in Birmingham. A number of project proposals for work in Israel had been under discussion in the office before he'd left for Tokyo. And an American electronics firm in Ireland seemed interested in receiving a proposal for production planning assistance. In any case, he'd ask for a week's leave in case Madeline was at the Nelson Column. They'd have time in London to get reacquainted. They'd also need the time to determine what to do next if she was going to apply for a junior product manager position at Marallon's Bond Street office.

He was still lost in thought as he reached the trattoria on Gloucester Terrace but stopped as the sidewalk chatter interrupted his thoughts. He sat down at an empty table not far from the door and ordered a bowl of chocolate ice cream.

Chapter 8

i

The next morning, John had time for a jog in Hyde Park, the first chance he'd had for over a month, and it felt good to work up a light sweat before the uneasy feeling in his right knee slowed him down.

After a shower, he headed down to the breakfast room, nodding to Pierre and Nicole Duval as he entered. He smiled good morning at Miss Brown as she handed him a menu.

Charley Smith passed close by with a hearty, "Glad to see you back, John."

John smiled and waved in return. After eating and passing Susanna Brice with a lazy "Morning" on his way out, John headed for the tube stop at Lancaster Gate. He had enough time to take it easy since his scheduled meeting with Tim Campbell was at 10:00 AM.

Marallon House's signature crimson door and the bright brass plate on the wall beside it gleamed in the morning sunlight and seemed to welcome him back as he touched the door bell button and pulled the door open. Smiling as usual, the receptionist replied that Mr. Campbell was in his office on the second floor. John switched his heavy briefcase to the other hand and walked to the lift.

Tim stood up and walked around his desk, right hand extended as John knocked and then walked through the open door.

"Glad to see you, John. Your time in Japan seems to have passed very quickly. Sit down," he said, motioning to a chair in front of the desk. "While you've been away, our launch of the new product line has been very successful. We're satisfied with the results."

"Sounds great."

"But, enough about our progress here in the UK. I hear from Kinya Arakawa that the Tokyo office is pleased with your draft report and that it seems to have settled the uneasiness that has been swirling around there for the past two years."

"Yes, I'm glad that it was a successful trip, Tim."

"In a nutshell, what did you find?"

"Well, the only thing that even remotely might have led to the death of one or more of the retailers was a procedural flaw in the billing and shipping process that might have led to a kickback scheme."

"That's unusual."

"It seemed like such an insignificant slip in the process, but I can understand that even a small amount of money is extremely important to a Japanese employee."

"When will we get the report?"

"Well, it's voluminous since it covers all the processes I reviewed and found OK, but it's reduced in an executive summary to a few paragraphs showing the procedural errors, or possible collusion, that might possibly have led to the murders."

"That's what we're all interested in."

"I'm taking the draft to our Worldwide London office in Bloomsbury this afternoon. I'll brief the head of our international projects group and have the draft finalized for approval by our executive. Copies will be sent to Marallon Tokyo and to Marallon House here. Final billing will be submitted when the report is accepted here at Marallon UK."

"Sounds fine, John. I'll inform our managing director of your plan, and I'll be looking forward to signing off on the report. Nice to have worked with you and Worldwide," said Tim with a smile as he stood up and extended his hand for a warm handshake.

John still had plenty of time before his next meeting, so he walked three offices down the hall and dropped in on Mike Ryan, the sales manager he had spent so much time with during his training program. Mike looked up and said enthusiastically, "Welcome back, John. How did the project go?"

"Just fine, Mike. The transpolar flights were really long and tiresome, but it's a far better way than going by ship. I'm glad I had worked in Japan before. It made things a lot easier for me.

I didn't find much in the way of problems, except one in the shipping and billing process, that may have led to the crimes."

"It's not hard to believe that something small could cause such a problem. Where are you headed now?"

"I'm on my way to our Worldwide office to make arrangements to finalize the report. Then it's back to Birmingham for the next assignment."

"Sounds great, John. Product demonstrations are helping the sell-through, and the brand is launching really successfully. Do you have time for a fast coffee?"

"Thanks, Mike, but I'd better get started for Bloomsbury. If there are any questions on the report, I'll be sure to answer them. If not, I'm not sure when I'll be back to Marallon House. Thanks again for all your help. Stop in to say hi next time you're in Birmingham."

"OK. Nice working with you, John."

ii

After a good-bye to the receptionist on his way out, John crossed Oxford Street and walked down into the Bond Street tube stop. Waiting for the train, he thought of Hannah, whom he'd be seeing the next day in Birmingham. She had sounded cool and somewhat aloof the last time he had called her from Tokyo. He knew that she was unhappy about his being away so long, but he had resigned himself to believing that his future with Worldwide would continue to take him to projects away from Birmingham, perhaps for long stretches of time.

Besides, he was missing Madeline more every day, and there was no way he could easily tell Hannah that he had fallen in love with another woman. It seemed best to tell Hannah that he felt that his future as a management consultant might continue to take him to faraway places, so it would be best if she didn't count on his being around as much as he had been in the past.

So, rather than let her life continue to slip away, waiting endlessly for his return, she might want to consider other opportunities for a loving relationship and a family life with children—whose father was working close by. He consoled himself by thinking that perhaps she had already considered this possibility, might have gone out with other chaps during their separation—but perhaps not. Their separation hadn't been exceptionally long, and she had never shown any inclination to want to date other men.

The train's arrival broke his concentration. With a heavy sigh, he took a seat and considered his coming meeting with the international projects director. He knew Bob Powell, had met him once, but his project in Japan was the first time that he'd worked overseas under his control.

Previous consulting assignments had been UK-oriented, and the details of the Marallon project had been worked out with Birmingham office management. He had every confidence that his report briefing would be well received. Lost in thought, he almost missed his stop at Holborn; after that it was only a short wait for the connecting train to Russell Square.

The last time he had been to Worldwide Consultants' building in Bloomsbury, he had been impressed with it, and he felt that way again as he walked in under the Worldwide Arch, the company's trademark.

A similar arch was constructed at Worldwide's Chicago office. He had seen pictures of it and hoped to get there one day, but now he was being directed to Bob Powell's office. The young woman who served as his staff assistant was sitting at the desk outside his office, and she announced John's arrival by phone. The director personally opened his door and invited John to a seat in front of his desk.

Without much small talk, the director remarked that he had seen John's draft summary from Tokyo. He knew that Kinya Arakawa was convinced the situation in Tokyo had been thoroughly examined and his concerns had been satisfied. John briefly restated the facts that he had presented to Tim Campbell at Marallon House, and then the director asked him to sit down with the report preparation team to arrange for finalizing the document.

It was past tea time when John and the team, led by Bob Powell's staff assistant, finished reviewing the draft in enough detail that he felt satisfied to start back to Beauregard House with a sigh of relief.

He called his home office in Birmingham and left word with the director's secretary that he'd be arriving after noon the next day to present a short overall briefing of the project, its findings, and the anticipated results.

Bob Powell had already left the office for the evening, so John confirmed with his assistant that he'd already arranged to be on leave for the next week, and then made his way back to the Russell Square tube stop.

It was a pleasant evening, and the walk was quiet; but the station was jammed, and a group of buskers banging away on their instruments could barely be heard as the train rolled up to the platform. John had to squeeze through the door, barely able to reach a hand strap; but he rode for only one stop, to Holburn, where he changed trains to the Central Line. That train was also crowded, and while it was only six stops to Lancaster Gate, John was glad that he was on his way back to Birmingham.

Walking up the steps to the Beauregard terrace, he pushed through the revolving door into the lobby just as final call for the evening meal was being announced. He stopped at the men's room to wash his hands and met Charley Smith just as he started into the dining room.

"This will be my last evening at Beauregard House for a while, Charley. Let's have dinner together."

"Fine, John. Where you headed? Back to Birmingham?"

"Yes. I've closed out my project here and am ready for a new assignment. How come you're eating so late this evening? You generally prefer your evening meal a bit earlier, as I recall."

"I do, but the agency has been finding more and more voice-over spots for me," he explained as they sat down at John's table.

"It's been making my schedule a bit irregular, but being retired, one of the things I have most is flexibility. Besides, the work seems to keep me moving from one ad agency to another, where there is always the possibility of meeting an attractive widow or even a not-so-young divorcée. It's going on two years since my wife Gwynne passed away, so women are beginning to look attractive to me again."

Taking the menu from John, who was giving his selection to Miss Brown, Charley made a quick choice and handed the menu to the waitress.

"Speaking of women," John said, "I had coffee last evening with Barbara and the colonel. They seemed pretty chummy."

"Yeah! I like her very much, but just because a man is attracted to a woman doesn't mean that the feeling is mutual. That's life. Not much I can do about it if she prefers a gray-haired military guy with a good posture instead of a balding widower with an ex-salesman's growing beer belly. I'll just continue to be friendly with everybody and keep my eye peeled for the next attractive widow."

"Do you think you have a better chance with a widow, rather than a divorcee or a single lady?" John asked.

"Yes, I do. The widow who's had a wonderful married life with a man she really loved may be so completely content with her family and her memories that she's just not ready for remarriage, but if a significant time has elapsed since his passing, she may begin to realize there's still time for love and affection—and life goes on."

"If, on the other hand, the husband had a bad time of it on his way to the grave, she may be very reluctant to have another old guy sitting around the house to feed and to clean up after, so in that case, chances may be nil."

"Seems like you've been giving widows some deep thought."

"Yes, I have—but one in particular. I've been thinking of Pamela. You may remember I mentioned her. Works at the

Corsair agency. I've been trying to talk to her every time I've had a chance, but she's always busy, can't stop to talk."

Nodding, John said, "Yes, I do remember you mentioning her."

"I still think she looks great. Not too tall, not too small. A pretty face with very few wrinkles, lovely dark eyes, wears red lipstick, gray hair always attractively neat, lovely breasts, each one a comfortable handful, I'd say. Reasonably flat stomach for one who's had three children, and not too heavy in the rear."

"Sounds like she has her curves in the right places."

"I'm not sure how old her children are, but sometimes, when the children are grown—even married—things become a little dicey if Momma starts to hint she's planning to invite John Doe for dinner some evening. I can almost hear the tone of their voices as they ask, 'Who's he? Why are you having him here? You haven't forgotten Dad already have you, Mother? I just wouldn't be able to think of another man as my father.' And the harried voice of the widow as she tries to explain, 'He's just a friend, and I'd like you to meet him.'"

"So, it may not be easy for a widow to get herself remarried even when she's beginning to think about the idea, especially if the kids are grown and worried about their inheritance."

"Got that right, Charley."

Picking up his fork and knife as his dinner plate was placed in front of him, Charley continued, "But getting back to divorcées, chances are, any attractive divorcée will be either feeling badly hurt because of something the husband did or feeling extremely angry over the break-up. In either case, she may be anxious to grab a new husband to prove she's still attractive and loved or to pay back her ex to show he was wrong about something."

"I see what you mean."

"Or, she may be so angry at men, I couldn't even talk to her without her blowing up. In the first case, I'm not too anxious to be grabbed as a husband because of some marital calamity. And in the second, there's not much chance for happiness or even for getting together until she cools down a while."

"I agree," John said with a nod.

"Of course, there's the odd chance she may be so relieved to be out of the marriage she'll be very receptive to a guy who's had a lifetime of happy marriage already. Like me, for example."

"Have you thought about finding a never-married gal?"

Nodding and forking another piece of chicken into his mouth, Charley mumbled, "The mature single woman is always a question mark. She may never have been asked, or she may be unwilling to marry, sometimes for religious (and sometimes for other) good reasons."

Swallowing, he went on, clarifying, "I really haven't found too many mature single ladies, or maybe I should say I haven't met many. In fact, there may not be too many around these days."

"Now that you mention it, I can't remember having met one in years." John added.

"Neither have I," Charley said, "It might be interesting to meet one and see what she thinks about a life together. I'd guess I'd know in a hurry if she was single because of strong religious beliefs of some kind, but if she's been caring for a sick mother or has lived in an isolated rural locality, it might be interesting. Hadn't thought about that before."

"Yeah, you may be surprised."

"Thanks for mentioning it, John. I'll keep my eyes open for the possibility." Forking the last piece of chicken into his mouth, Charley asked, "What about your situation with women?"

Finishing his last forkful of spaghetti, John put his knife and fork together on his plate and pushed it back a few inches. He wiped his lips on his napkin, dropped it back in his lap, looked over at the older man, and said, "Well, I've been seriously fond of a young lady in Birmingham for about a year, but we've had some difficulties that have me thinking that we're really not well suited for each other. Since I've been away, I've missed her, but at the same time, since I've been here I've met Madeline. And even though I haven't known her long, we both feel very attracted to each other. She's been away for weeks giving cosmetics demonstrations, but you may remember her."

As Charley nodded, John continued, "She also has romantic commitments—back in Brighton. Madeline and I seem very compatible, and if we can each untangle ourselves from our present relationships, we'll meet again here in London to see if we can figure out a way to put our lives together."

"Good luck to both of you," Charley said and smiled. "Let's have coffee in the lounge."

iii

John checked out of the Beauregard early the next morning, and he was a bit sorry he hadn't seen Barbara or Glenn Johnson in the lounge the previous evening or at breakfast. He liked them both and had wanted to say his farewells. *Can't win 'em all*, he thought as the cab took him to the railway station.

The train ride was less than three hours, just about the same time as driving the 154 miles from London to Birmingham, and it was more relaxing, too. He hadn't slept well last night, and now the thoughts of his next, and perhaps last, meeting with Hannah were tumbling around in his brain again.

As he thought of the many wonderful experiences they'd had together, he felt deeply disturbed at the thought of not seeing her anymore. Sitting quietly on the train, smoking his pipe, he felt their good times together had clearly overshadowed their problems.

Thoughts of seeing Madeline again frequently popped into his thoughts, only to be chased away by visions of Hannah that returned again and again. She had wanted to meet him at the station, but he had demurred, saying he wasn't sure of his arrival time.

He knew the conversation might not be too pleasant, and he'd rather meet her at his place in a quiet setting. But that didn't seem very practical now. He glanced at his watch; it was close to noon, so she'd be on her way to lunch with an office friend. Better to meet her after work, have a chatty dinner, and then go back to his place.

Even that would be dicey. If she became extremely angry, it would certainly be difficult driving her home. Far better to suggest going back to her place after dinner. If the parting wasn't pleasant and friendly as he hoped, he could at least leave at the right time.

As the train slowed, John lifted his luggage from the overhead rack, thinking again that he was glad to have located an apartment on Vincent Drive not far from the station. It had been convenient to have one so close to Birmingham University during the time he'd worked on his degree in the graduate program at the business school.

Opening the door and stepping into his apartment, he felt the dry, dusty air on his face, clear evidence that he'd not been there since early summer. He dropped his luggage, quickly opened the windows facing the street and the bedroom windows facing the park, and was relieved to feel the light, refreshing breeze as it stirred the curtains.

He was glad he'd thought to grab a sandwich on the train since there seemed to be lots to do. He unpacked his suitcase, piled the dirty laundry in a heap on top of the washer, called his mother in Stourbridge, quickly grabbed a dust cloth, and whisked the most prominent places clean. He closed the windows, reached for his briefcase, and left the apartment to check in at Worldwide's Birmingham office.

As he expected, there were only a few consultants in the office, finalizing reports or writing proposals; the rest were on assignment somewhere, so he had enough time to thoroughly brief the director on the Marallon project.

Afterward, he shook hands with everyone in the office and sat down at his desk. He called Hannah and arranged to pick her up. He prepared a file for his own draft copy of the Marallon report, quickly reviewed the last two monthly summary reports of office activities and events, scanned possible project assignments awaiting his return from next week's leave, and stopped to cash a check at the same bank where Hannah worked.

iv

Hannah had missed John terribly during the first three or four weeks that he'd been in London. They had been so close during his early consulting assignments around Birmingham, and she'd needed him close during almost all of her free time. There really hadn't been any specific reason, but she felt so lonely without him. She knew it had been difficult for him since he never seemed to have enough free time to do the research he had needed to do in order to prepare new proposals for Worldwide.

She could tell he'd been annoyed, even though they had never seemed to quite come to an all-out argument over her almost never-ending demands that he be close at hand. But, their relationship seemed to have cooled during his first few weeks in London, and even more so as his time away had stretched into months.

At first, she had been resentful, at times angry, about their separation, but as her time at her new job had passed, she seemed more confident in herself and in her capability to do excellent work. Her confidence in herself seemed to give her courage to respond as the young currency trader, who also worked at ING

Direct, stopped to chat with her when they occasionally met in the bank elevator.

George was not as good-looking as John, but she liked his curly dark hair and his wry sense of humor. By now she was starting to feel comfortable with him since he worked on the second floor and she worked four floors above.

Now, as she locked her desk, she felt nervous about seeing John again. She said good night to the few women who hadn't yet left the office, stopped in the ladies' room to freshen up, and took the elevator to the lobby.

John was waiting for her, standing about midway between the revolving doors and the elevators. Breaking into a big smile as she hurried toward him, he was pleased at her bright, happy look, her tailored yellow blouse and light-brown skirt blending nicely with her blond hair.

They met in a tight hug, arms wrapped around each other, her breasts tightly pressed to his chest. Their lips met solidly in a long, passionate kiss, the long separation, the annoyances, forgotten in an instant.

"Oh, I'm so happy to see you, John."

"You look wonderful, Hannah. I've missed you so much."

She said, "You've been away so long, and there seems to be so much to talk about. But not much has happened here, not much change in my life. I seem to be doing well at my new job, but you've seen so much, I want to hear all about it."

Taking her hand, he said, "The car's parked up the street. Let's go to Antonio's for red wine and spaghetti." They started toward the revolving doors.

It was a long and happy dinner for both of them as John told of his travels in Scotland and Ireland before his departure for Japan, his experience in returning to Tokyo, and the success of the Marallon project.

He talked a bit about expected assignments after he returned to the office, that he'd be in London for the following week, that there was a good chance that he'd be assigned on another Far East project, putting together a proposal for a management study of the Rubber Industry Smallholders Development Authority in Kuala Lumpur, Malaysia.

She grew quiet as he talked more about the future, about being away again, for weeks, perhaps another month, perhaps much longer. They returned to her apartment, but the conversation in the car seemed to bring less and less of a response from Hannah as John tried to keep the subjects light. The uncertainty of the future hung like a heavy cloud between them. He suggested as lightly as he could that life was too short for her to lose opportunities for an interesting life by just sitting at home waiting for his return, that he'd be unhappy asking her to wait indefinitely as his career stretched off into the world of international business consulting.

The more he spoke to Hannah of the future of his profession, the more he became convinced that he was making the right decision to suggest that she begin to widen her circle of friends, to begin to consider going out with other men. It was a very subdued departure as he kissed her good night at her front door. They both seemed so depressed at the thought of parting, of not really wanting to think of the future. Their fun reunion had dribbled downhill to a somber, unhappy departure as the uncertainties of the future crowded in on them.

Driving back to his apartment, John found he'd hardly been able to say the words and had begun subconsciously to realize that his relationship with Madeline would also be in jeopardy due to the long project assignments that might keep them apart for what might seem like unbearably long periods of time.

The relative uncertainties of the consulting profession, the need for continuous preparation of proposals, the constant marketing, and then the skillful search for the right solutions for management problems were the constant pressures that made it a challenging and exciting field of endeavor.

The next morning, Friday 30 August, John checked in at Worldwide's Birmingham office and joined the small team that was beginning to pull together ideas for the Kuala Lumpur proposal. The preliminary draft proposal would soon be transferred to the international team in London, but for John it was a one-day assignment since he would be on leave beginning on Monday and could possibly be assigned to a different project upon his return.

That evening, he joined his mother for dinner at her home in Stourbridge. She was quite fond of Hannah and was very sorry to hear John's suggestion that Hannah make every attempt to broaden her circle of friends, including beginning to date other men. John had been impatient with Hannah's dependence on him, but during lunches with Hannah during John's trip to Japan, John's mother had felt that Hannah's self-confidence had improved considerably. But during his work for Marallon in London, John had mentioned his meeting Madeline to his mother, so, in a way, she was pleased to hear that John was looking forward to seeing Madeline in London again.

Chapter 9

i

Sunday, 1 September, the date that Madeline had agreed to meet him at the Nelson Column in Trafalgar Square—provided that she and her boyfriend Wendell had agreed to end their relationship amiably. John was up early as usual, did his morning exercises, and had a leisurely breakfast. He grabbed his packed suitcase, locked it in his car, and headed for the M40 with plenty of time to get to London. He turned onto the M42 near Bromsgrove then onto the M40 at the first intersection, headed southeast past Warwick on the way to Oxford.

It was a pleasant morning, but traffic seemed heavier than usual. He lit a cigarette, settled back a bit more comfortably in the driver's seat, and wondered how Madeline had managed what he hoped were her final hours with Wendell. Many times he'd wished he and Madeline had agreed to write during their time apart. It had seemed like a good idea at the time not to communicate—to give each of them time to rethink their attachment to each other and to resolve their relationships independently.

But it had been a very difficult time for him—wondering whether Madeline had been able to join the marketing team at Marallon, whether she'd still find him attractive, whether they'd easily be able to recapture the warm, loving relationship that had developed between them during their time at Gram's and their hours together in London. Would she be there waiting for him or would he have to wait in agony, not knowing whether she'd show up?

The time seemed to drag by; a minute seemed like ten. He was driving the speed limit, and he did his best to focus on the road ahead instead of the uncertainty that faced him at Nelson's Column. For whatever reason, he failed to see the heavily loaded truck, unusual in Sunday morning traffic, trying to change lanes behind him by sliding between the cars that were preventing the driver from reaching the M20 exit at Banbury.

John barely caught a glimpse of the truck in his right-hand mirror as the driver tried to slow the heavily loaded vehicle. It rammed into the back end of his car and slammed it off the road where it flipped over, the back wheels hitting the soft shoulder.

ii

In London, Madeline walked slowly between two of the huge cast bronze lions that formed the large square around the base of the Nelson Column. She couldn't sit still; she'd tried it for a while, sitting on the highest step around the base of the column, but was so nervous that she had to get up and keep moving.

There was lots of activity in Trafalgar Square that morning: children climbing up on the lions' backs, kids wading in the fountains and pools, heavy traffic along the street in front of the National Gallery, tourists feeding the pigeons.

The activity was little more than a distraction to Madeline as she waited impatiently, but serenely, her head turning ceaselessly as her eyes scanned the crowds for that first sign of John. She had been there since 11:30, but each minute had seemed like ten. There was really no reason to be concerned, she thought.

It wasn't clear where he'd be coming from, but instinctively, she knew he must be coming from Birmingham since she had heard from Louisa Hastings at the ad agency that the Marallon project had been completed.

She thought back, with pleasure, to her time with John, the visit to Gram's in Cambridge, their museum crawling around London, flashbacks to their ice cream breaks at the trattoria and their meals together at Beauregard House.

Less pleasantly, her thoughts slid toward her last hours with Wendell. Last weekend, she had been visiting her parents in Brighton, but she had been uneasy about her coming date with Wendell on Saturday night.

After she had finished her promotional tours for Marallon's new product introductions, she had left Beauregard House and had moved into Louisa Hasting's spare bedroom temporarily, so she had not been back in Brighton for some time. Her long discussions with her mother and dad on Friday evening, and then again over Saturday morning breakfast, had been tense.

It had been difficult for her parents to reconcile with the fact that Madeline had reached the point where she was ready to leave the family nest in Brighton, to leave her modeling work and embark on a new business career in London. They had realized their daughter's relationship with Wendell had cooled considerably during her long promotional tours for Marallon, but they hadn't known of his sometimes almost violent possessiveness toward her. Now, as she explained her uneasiness regarding ending the relationship, and her happiness at the idea of seeing John again, they too had mixed emotions over her date with Wendell.

She glanced at her watch. The time seemed to be going so slowly. *Where could he be?* Her mind slid back to the previous weekend in Brighton.

She had been busy all afternoon. It was the perfect opportunity to sort out the clothes she wanted to take to her room at Louisa's flat. There were so many things, far too much to take with her in two suitcases on the train, but she managed to sort out the best of her workday clothing to take with her on her return to London on Sunday.

Louisa's offer to drive down to Brighton the following weekend would certainly help to move most of her clothes to London; but there wasn't much closet space, so lots of off-season stuff would just have to wait until later. And Louisa's offer to have Madeline share the flat had been a real lifesaver. Due to her lack of marketing experience, her starting salary as an assistant product manager in Marallon's marketing department was so low that she wouldn't have been able to take the job unless she'd found someone to share a flat. And rents in the West End were high too.

Madeline felt that time was closing in on her. One more week until the first of September. It had seemed so far away at first, and the months had passed so slowly; but now, with only one more week until her meeting with John, after months of being apart, she felt more and more anxious, and that evening's date with Wendell was sure to be difficult. She could barely keep her mind on what she was doing.

She hadn't known Wendell very long. She had met him on one of her photo assignments. In fact, he was the insurance agent who had helped settle the case when Aaron the photographer had died during the horrible accident on the photo shoot. *Was it only eight months ago?* she wondered. It seemed much longer ago than that.

Wendell had been very helpful in handling the problems between the ad agency and the furniture manufacturing company and the claims over responsibilities involved in the accident. He had been infatuated with her from the very beginning, but she wasn't too happy about his choice of places to go during their dates. Going to the Brighton Centre or the Nightingale Theatre had been OK, and visits to the Duke of York's Picturehouse had been fun. But there seemed to be too many unsavory places that Wendell wanted to take her.

She had been born and raised in Brighton, but as she grew up, Brighton's reputation became more and more distasteful to her parents, and to her and her brother as well. Wendell persisted in wanting to take her to places said to be patronized by members of the lesbian, gay, bisexual, and transgender communities, and she had consented to go a few times; but her refusal frequently ended with their attending the Brighton Dome or the Theatre Royal.

Wendell seemed to think that just because she was a model and was accustomed to working in an advertising agency's photographic environment that she enjoyed the nightclub atmosphere, where sexual mores were considerably looser than average—but she didn't, not at all—and she found it annoying that he persisted in suggesting they go to such places.

Now that she had accepted the position with Marallon in London and was looking forward to living in the West End and the challenge of beginning the development of a new young woman's fragrance line, she wanted to break off her dating with Wendell and think about a new relationship with John.

It wasn't that she was afraid of Wendell, but he was so possessive; seemed to feel he owned her; tried to tell her what to do; tried to insist on doing what he wanted without considering her desires. He was nice-looking and could be charming at times, but he tried to force himself on her with too much hugging and overly passionate kissing, putting his hands on her breasts, her legs—being far too aggressive.

She had agreed to have dinner with him on the pier that night, knowing she could take a cab home from there if the evening ended unpleasantly. She wanted to have a quiet dinner since it would be the last one.

Wendell had been glad to see her, had grabbed her, and kissed her passionately as they got into his car at her home. As usual, he'd come in to shake hands with her dad and assure him he'd have Madeline home early. He'd been talkative about his work and had chattered on about missing her as they drove to the pier.

He'd tried to convince her to stop at one of the clubs, and her insistence had almost ended in an argument; but she'd won, and once they arrived at the restaurant, they talked casually about news events and happenings at Downing Street.

The restaurant was noisy and casual, just the kind of non-romantic setting that Madeline had wanted. Wendell had not been happy about her choice, and he seemed less talkative as she chatted on about her new job, her happiness about moving into Louisa's flat, and her job opportunities with Marallon.

Wendell seemed to have difficulty understanding she was trying to say good-bye and that this was going to be their last date. Before she had gotten the job with Marallon doing the promotional appearances for the new product launch, they had dated every weekend, and now that the promotions had ended, he had expected to resume their regular meetings.

Some of their times together had not been as pleasant as he'd liked, but he'd felt most comfortable and relaxed with her. During her absence from Brighton, he had gone out with other women, mostly those he'd met casually at various clubs, but none of them had been more than two or three unromantic dates. The women had seemed to be less interested in a close relationship, and he seemed to be drifting toward the casual sex scene, which didn't fit in with his own opinion of himself as a responsible member of the insurance community.

It finally began to sink in. He had almost tuned her out as she spoke softly about her future in London. He was losing her. He couldn't quite believe that he wouldn't be seeing her anymore. *I've lost her*, he said to himself. A feeling, an unexplainable feeling, not of panic, not loneliness, just a feeling of loss ran through his mind.

He hardly knew what he was eating. He realized her move from Brighton was taking her out of his life. So, arguments against the move, arguments for occasional dates in London, welled up in his throat as he pleaded for reconsideration, knowing only too well that he was not convincing her to change her mind. He couldn't believe it was over. Mechanically, he reached for his wallet as the waiter handed him the bill.

They drove back to her home in near-complete silence. He told her how much he loved her, how sorry he was they were breaking up.

"I can hardly believe it," he said again.

She kissed him for the last time as she opened the car door and almost breathed a sigh of relief as she walked up to the front door. It had been difficult, and she'd had some regrets as the last week before the first of September slid by very slowly, almost hour by hour.

She looked at her watch. She had been deeply lost in thought, and now it was almost 12:30. She had almost forgotten where she was as she looked around and found herself sitting quietly at the foot of Nelson's Column. Almost in panic, she stood up walked quickly around the four lions looking almost frantically for John. Nothing. She walked around again and looked at her watch again.

Something must have happened. She felt strongly, deep inside, that John would have been there if he had been able. She had requested and received special permission to have the coming week as personal time, and she didn't doubt that she'd be able to go back to work on Monday morning.

The folks at Marallon had been helpful as she relocated from Brighton, and she felt confident that the director of the marketing department would understand her desire to postpone her request for personal time. She had been closemouthed about her reason for needing the time just in case something like this happened.

She walked around the four lions many more times. A gnawing remembered thought began to creep into her mind. John had set the date that they would meet in Trafalgar Square. He had also set one condition: each of them should think seriously of their commitments and meet only if previous commitments had been seriously considered and ended. That gave each of them a way out in case either one should reconsider.

Was it possible that John had changed his mind—had been unable to end his prior commitment to Hannah in Birmingham? No, he wouldn't leave her standing there alone after a three-hour wait because he didn't feel committed to her. No, it wasn't possible, or was it?

She wasn't sure. She wouldn't try to find out from his mother in Birmingham—just in case. She'd feel grossly insulted if she found that John was there in Birmingham, that he hadn't planned to be in London on that day.

There really were two options—first, he had been unable to be there, and second, he had changed his mind and chosen to not be there. Which was it? She'd wait and see what happened.

iii

John woke up in a bed in Trinity Hospital in Banbury. He didn't know he was in Banbury until the nurse heard his soft groan, noticed he was awake, and answered his question about where he was.

He had been badly injured when his car had rolled over after being pushed off the M40 by the heavy truck. The nurse explained that his mother and Worldwide Consultants had been notified after he had come out of the operating room. He had been identified by the documents he had been carrying. The nurse knew he was in pain but explained that, now that he was conscious, the doctor would be in shortly with medication to help deal with it. He had been unconscious for three days, and his mother had been in to see him; she would return now that he was awake, as soon as the doctor would permit it. The nurse couldn't give him any specific idea about his injuries, about what was broken or damaged. He was heavily bandaged with some splints, but he'd learn more as soon as the doctor arrived.

"Well, here he is now."

"Hello there. I'm Dr. Evans. Don't try to talk much yet. Now that you're awake, I'll prescribe pain medication that the nurse will help you with. You've had us worried. You'll be with us for a while unless you'd rather be transferred elsewhere, but we can discuss that later. After my examination, we'll see if we can get you to eat something. If it's too difficult, we'll continue feeding you intravenously for a few days. I'll give you an overview of your problems, but we'll have a better idea of your condition over the next few days. Now, let's take a look at your head."

To John, the hours, the days, seemed to move agonizingly slowly. He'd asked to be partly sedated rather than lie there unable to move much of his body, unable to bring his mind to focus on his condition, unable to think about the future, unable to decide what to do about Madeline.

His mother and Hannah had been in to see him every few days, and he seemed to be making some progress as his sharp pains subsided into unpleasant aches. Sedated sleep seemed to be the best cure for the internal damage and for the injuries to sections of his back.

Now that he'd been assured the truck company's insurance would continue to pay his hospital and convalescence expenses, and that Worldwide's insurance coverage included his salary so his rent would be assured, he was able to relax enough to perform the physical therapy exercises that were helping to bring feeling and capability into his legs. There was also every reason to believe the weakness in his spine would eventually heal as his cracked vertebrae recovered.

As the weeks dragged into two months, he was finally able to start thinking about the future. After he had moved out of the hospital into the assisted living facility in Birmingham, the physical therapy sessions had taken so much of his time, and so much energy, that there had been no time to really think about the future. It had been an exhausting experience.

Hannah's first offer to assist him to get away from the facility, to attend a musical play in Birmingham, had been both difficult and painful for both of them. For her part, after a number of unsuccessful and embarrassing starts, she finally had accepted his suggestion that she begin dating other men, and to her surprise, she had been happily successful in meeting a number of young accountants and engineers, primarily where she worked. Nevertheless, John's miserable physical condition and their closeness in the past had been such that she felt a strong willingness to help him take the first steps toward a normal life.

The crutches had been difficult, and the wheelchair had been inconvenient at times; but together, including John's full dependence on Hannah, the exact opposite of their previous relationship, they managed to overcome John's transport problems as they enjoyed a few of Birmingham's early season's musicals and dramas.

As his physical condition improved, he began to be concerned about his ability to make a living. The convalescence assistance was almost finished, and his sick time allowance at Worldwide would be ending; but he'd been assured by Arnold Nesbitt, manager of Worldwide Consultants' Birmingham office that a project assignment would be waiting for him as soon as he was ready.

iv

In London, Madeline's preliminary creative ideas for development of Marallon's new line of fragrances aimed at Britain's younger women had been tentatively approved by Tim Campbell. With the concurrence of Marallon's budget director, she and Don Wilson, a budget analyst, visited the office of Spectre Fragrances in Birmingham. It was a specialty house that had utilized its technical expertise to develop a line of chemical fragrance products.

Madeline opened the conversation with George Schwartz, president of the company. "Marallon would like to explore use of your firm as an outsource to develop a new set of fragrance products for younger women under the Marallon brand."

"Marallon doesn't have the expertise or the production facilities available to create the product line for which I, as the product manager, have responsibility."

Taking a copy of the letter from her purse, she said, "As Marallon's marketing director's letter explains, my purpose over the next few days is to work closely with your experts and craftsmen to develop tentative ideas for new fragrance products that will encourage the younger generation of women to use scented products in new and creative ways."

Holding up a brooch, she went on, "Some examples include hair ornaments, brooches, and similar jewelry, necklaces, and unconventional items. Relatively small production runs are planned to determine how well the new products are accepted in selected test markets."

On their way back to the hotel late that afternoon, Madeline was elated with the reception they'd received, the quality of possible samples they'd seen, and the enthusiasm of the designers and mechanics they'd met. She had been impressed with how Don Wilson's cost-oriented questions during the meetings had helped to focus the discussions on both creative and financial cooperation with Spectre.

Later, as they had agreed, Madeline met Don in the hotel lobby, feeling quite pleased, ravenously hungry for dinner, and looking forward to an evening at the Theatre. The play, *Look Homeward, Angel*, had been revived in London's Repertoire Theatre last year and had just moved to Birmingham after a very successful run. The fact that the tickets had been presented to them as a gift from Spectre's president had added to the pleasure of the evening.

The play had been delightful; the seats were down front but not too close to the stage. Madeline and Don sat and quietly savored the moment. The cast had taken its final bows to thunderous applause, and the final curtain had come down. It was time to join the crowd. Making their way up the aisle, Madeline stopped dead. She wasn't quite sure, but she thought she saw John McKay sitting in an aisle seat, talking casually with a blonde sitting next to him.

People coming up from behind, pushed around her as she leaned over and said, "Hello, John. It's Madeline Claiborne. Nice to see you. It's been a long time. How are you?"

He looked up, startled and caught completely off guard. He hesitated and then looked at her more closely, slowly recognizing her.

"Madeline. What a surprise!" He made no attempt to get up. The noise of the crowd and the press of people trying to get past prevented any conversation. She glanced over at the blonde and succumbed to the pressure of those behind her.

With a wave of her hand, she said, "Nice to see you again, John," and then moved on up the aisle. Badly shaken, her mind in turmoil, she thought, *He looks about the same as I remember. Why didn't he meet me at Trafalgar Square as he promised? Was the blonde his old girlfriend?* She had to see him again, to find out what had happened.

As they reached the back of the theater and the crowd thinned a bit, Don said, "That chap looked familiar. Seems to me I remember seeing him in Marallon House some time ago."

"Yes, you did," she answered. "He worked on a training project there, then went off to Japan. That's the first I've seen him since his return."

She let it go at that. She changed the subject to their experience at Spectre that day and began to talk about plans for the next day's meetings.

They didn't stop for a snack after the show, and after a quick good night in the hotel lobby, Madeline went right to her room, her mind crowded with thoughts of John, their times together, and the deep feelings of love and affection that were rekindled by the sight of him again. She was sure he had felt the same when he departed for Japan. She just knew it, and she was certain that something must have prevented his getting to Trafalgar Square.

Sitting down at the table, she reached for the Birmingham city phone book and found his name, address, and phone number. Hesitating, her hand reached toward the phone. She paused and glanced at her watch. No, it was too late to call tonight. She dropped the phone back onto the cradle, put both hands to her forehead, closed her eyes, and ran her hands across her eyebrows. She gave a long sigh. She looked into the mirror and reached for the comb on the table.

Slowly combing her hair, she hoped that she'd be able to sleep that night, but finally her mind drifted back to the second round of designs she wanted to talk about at tomorrow morning's meeting. Reaching for her briefcase, she pulled out her sketchbook and was soon immersed in design concepts that finally helped her drift off to sleep.

V

Madeline had decided to call John before breakfast in the hope of catching him, possibly before he'd be leaving for work, so breakfast in the hotel was rushed the next morning. But she and Don were still on time for their meeting at Spectre at eight thirty.

She had decided to avoid getting into a long conversation with him over the phone and just arrange to meet that evening. He had sounded pleased to hear from her and suggested that she come to his place after work at Spectre. She thought they could meet someplace for dinner, but he suggested that she come right up to his apartment and walk right on in—the door would be open.

She had asked for help in finding the address, so she had no trouble in locating it. There wasn't much parking available, but with a bit of luck, she was able to find a place within short walking distance. She was glad now that she had been authorized to drive a Marallon company car on this working assignment.

It had been another very busy and productive day at Spectre, but now, as she stepped out of the car, locked the car door, and moved toward the sidewalk and the address up the street, an idea crossed her mind: perhaps she had been wrong; perhaps John had intentionally chosen to avoid meeting her in Trafalgar Square; perhaps he'd chosen to return to his girlfriend when he completed the project in Japan.

Perhaps she should say she was sorry she hadn't gone to the agreed meeting place and see what he would say. At least, she wouldn't feel foolish if he hadn't intended to meet her.

She didn't notice it was a beautiful summer evening, the sun moving toward a picturesque sunset as she walked to the apartment building entrance. The elevator was waiting; the ride to the third floor was smooth.

Madeline walked slowly down the hall, stopped at number 303, and took a deep breath. She knocked on the door, reached for the doorknob, pulled the door open, and walked in.

It was a large, pleasant room, and John was sitting in a chair by the windows. He folded the newspaper he was reading, dropped it on the table beside him, and with a broad smile, extended his arms.

"Madeline. How very nice to see you." She walked over and took his hands in hers when he didn't get up.

"Hello, John. It seems like such a long time."

"Please sit down," he said, motioning to a nearby chair.

"You'll have to excuse me for not getting up; I'm still not steady on my feet, but that's a long story. Tell me, whatever happened to the job opportunity at Marallon, and what are you doing in Birmingham?"

She was breathing more easily now. He looked just about the same, his tousled hair, his broad and ready smile, his soft but firm voice.

She started speaking slowly about her experience during the closing days of her product introduction appearances, her early interviews with Tim Campbell and others in the marketing department.

He didn't say anything, just smiled and looked at her, his blue eyes holding hers.

She hesitated, continued speaking slowly, very quietly, about her move to London and sharing an apartment with Louisa Hastings, being hired as an assistant product manager.

He nodded frequently, listening carefully, clearly pleased with watching her but not interrupting.

She paused, her mind racing, wanting to ask why he hadn't shown up in Trafalgar Square, but she didn't. Instead, she continued, carefully choosing her words, about her work with other product managers and the advertising agency.

Finally, he said, "Sounds terrific, but what are you doing in Birmingham?"

Still not feeling at ease, she spoke with more confidence about her ideas for new fragrance products and closed with her experience at Spectre.

As she talked, he realized how very much he had missed her, how long it had been; his mind went back to his project time in Tokyo, his short time back in Worldwide's Birmingham office, the accident, and the long recovery time.

She was just as beautiful as he remembered her, and she spoke so well. Her streaked blonde hair almost reached her shoulders. As she spoke, she occasionally crossed her legs; her body moved, and the pale yellow blouse revealed her youthful curves, as he had remembered them.

"You've done very well," he said, "and you're just as beautiful as you were when we kissed at Beauregard House and said, 'Until next time we meet.'"

"Yes," she said, "and that was scheduled to be on September first." Then, still not sure why he hadn't been there, she looked at him and said slowly, "I'm sorry I didn't make it to Trafalgar Square that day. I didn't know how to reach you, so I had no alternative. Did you wait for me a long time?"

He looked stunned, shook his head slowly, and looked at her.

"No, I didn't wait because I wasn't able to make it there. I was thinking about our meeting, perhaps driving too fast, and wasn't paying enough attention to my driving or I might have been able to avoid the truck that caused the accident. I was unconscious for three days before I woke up in a hospital bed. I didn't attempt to reach you because I was so badly hurt that I wasn't sure I'd ever be able to work again, and I didn't want you to feel obligated in any way."

Now crying, her face displaying her anguish, she dropped to her knees in front of him and reached up to his face with both hands.

"I was lying; I was there and waited for three hours until I realized that something must have happened. I wasn't sure if you'd changed your mind and decided to not meet me. Oh, John, I wish I'd known. I'd have been here months ago—to help, to love you as I did before you left for Japan. I've been so miserable thinking that you had changed your mind—that you didn't want me.

Now in tears, he held her face in both of his hands and covered her lips, her cheeks, her eyes with kisses.

"Oh, Madeline, I do love you, and I'm almost well enough to go back to work. I'm sure we'll have a happy future together."

vi

John McKay walked up out of the underground at Russell Square station and headed for Worldwide Consultants' London office in Bloomsbury. He stopped to light a cigarette, thought better of it, and shoved the pack back into his shirt's breast pocket. He had almost given up the habit. The pipe was long gone, but he occasionally had to fight off the temptation to light up a cigarette.

Today was to be his first day in the London office, so it had been a reasonable temptation, he thought.

Everything had gone so quickly: his final days on crutches, his return to work in Birmingham, his re-assignment from the project in Kuala Lumpur to the chamber of commerce project in Curacao, with temporary transfer to the London office. He was back at Beauregard House again for a few weeks and still had to find a place to live, but now that Madeline was sharing a flat with Louisa in Chelsea, he could hardly believe his good luck. He turned right at the next corner and saw the golden arch of the Worldwide Consultants sign straight ahead. He walked up to the revolving door, pushed through, and walked into his next consulting engagement.

About the Author

William Lyster lives in St. Petersburg, Florida. He served as personal assistant to the chairman, international, of one of America's most prestigious pharmaceutical companies, followed by training in Europe before assignment as general manager of consumer product subsidiaries in Canada and then Japan. He was also vice president of a Chicago-based international management consulting firm.